Once in A Blue Moon

HAILEE PRESSER

Third Edition

ISBN: 9798596863574

Author's Note

This is actually version 3 of *The Shifters of Salem.*

I started this series at the age of twelve, and, after getting it published, realized I wasn't quite happy with it. It has since been reworked, but still retains the story I told all those years ago. If you have an original copy of the book from when it was first released way back in 2017, I just want to say thank you for supporting me and watching me continue to learn, improve, and grow as a young author and artist.

Hi, Mimo!

Table of Contents

1
OLIVER
Things get problematic

I was *not* thrilled. "A problem? We just fixed the problem. There can't be a problem, that's problematic," I said, talking a mile a minute.

"Well, there is," said Zade.

"But how? If we got rid of Derek and Kyra, how can there be another one?" Juniper wondered.

"Who says we got rid of them," said Zade.

Now my weirdness meter was going berserk. It was off the charts. How could they have survived Zade's magic explosion of fire and *still* want to come back for more? I was far enough away from Zade and Juniper when it happened, and even I got knocked back on my butt.

"So, what happens when you finally do fix the problem then?" asked Juniper. "That's it? You just...... disappear?"

A small square in the floor that served as the entrance to the attic lifted up, unfolding stairs below. Ralph emerged into the attic, closing the hatch behind him.

"No. As long as the Zenith is alive, he will do what he has been made to do. The Zenith is an omen from the Sky Fire; a message from Anput," Ralph explained. "When one dies, another will be born, and he or she will grow up to pick up where the last one left off."

"You have a knack for showing up out of nowhere and answering questions, don't you?" said Zade.

"It's one of my hobbies; the other being golf."

"How do you know how all this works?" I wondered.

"I know more than you think I do," said Ralph. "I... I had a son, but he was brutally torn from my grasp. We didn't get along the best, and I never got a chance to tell him how much he meant to me. After his death, I've tried countless times to call upon him in the Sky Fire, but I've never gotten anywhere with it. My son was a Zenith. My son was William."

"*Oh, waah!*" screamed Lycan, "*He had it comin'!*"

"Ralph, I–" started Juniper.

"It's quite all right, Juniper. I just don't want Zade to suffer the same fate as my poor William. But I understand you need to talk with your friends, and I'll go if you wish..." Ralph grabbed the small knob on the hatch and opened it.

"Ralph, wait," said Zade.

Ralph stopped and looked at him.

"So, you're a Council member. You've got the tattoo and everything. Why can't you stop the other members and packs from wanting me dead?"

"I've tried. I've tried so hard. But Raoul and Asena agreed, and it's two against one. They wouldn't listen to me. Many other Zeniths have been killed off due to their orders. William was the only exception because he was my son, and they thought I would be able to watch his actions. Council members are rarely in the same place at the same time, and the only times we ever meet is in Nome, Alaska, to discuss important matters. I'm stationed here, in Salem, Oregon, Raoul in Salem, New Jersey, and Asena in Salem, Massachusetts. I've been able to keep you a secret from them so far, but Zade, if you go to Massachusetts, there will be nothing I can do for you anymore."

"Then that's a risk I'll have to be willing to take," said Zade.

"Then I have no right to stand in your way." Ralph began to climb down the ladder. "I'm off to town. We're running low on supplies and food. I'll be back in an hour." Then he closed the door after him.

"Onto the bigger, more recent issue here," I said. "What's the dream?"

"Um, yeah. I think we deserve some answers," Juniper demanded. She was wearing a red shirt and denim jeans, now paired with Lycan's golden chain necklace with the swirled charm dangling from the necklace chain. Her loose blond curls fell neatly in place on her shoulders.

"I don't fully understand it myself," confessed Zade, "but, before I woke up, I was in a dream-like state. I had no idea what was happening beyond what I was seeing. The outside world didn't seem to exist."

"Well, what did you see?" pushed Juniper.

"I saw a full moon, and it was glowing blue around the edges. Derek was there, too."

"What was he doing?" Juniper nudged, trying to get more information out of her boyfriend.

"I don't know... being stupid? He had a black mist swirling around him," Zade recalled. "I remember feeling like I wasn't alone, like there was another presence."

"Nice detective work, Sherlock!" screeched Lycan from inside his wolf shaped obsidian rock prison. *"Now we totally know what's happening! I see no way how this could possibly go wrong!"*

"Great," I sighed, throwing my hands up in despair. "So, we have a fiery friend, a very mean rock, and an enemy that refuses to die. Just once I'd like to be able to go to the movies without having their fantasy be my reality. Just once!"

"Just be thankful that the Hunger Games is not your reality," said Juniper.

"Unfortunately, my reality is with you two crazy people, and we spend our time fixing problems," I complained. "And, as it turns out, the problem just so happens to be Mr. Magic's family."

"Family issues, am I right?" shrugged Zade.

2
ZADE

Lost: my marbles.
Reward if found.

I had had a strange day. The vision thing was the worst of it. I had no idea what it meant. After all, I'm the only one who's supposed to do 'magic,' if you can even call it that. Firepower, or whatever. But how could Derek have had that black mist then? I'm the Zenith and even *I* can't do that.

I'd just have to wait and figure it out. That's usually what happened anyways. At least someone had been kind enough to put me in my trusty green Oregon Ducks sweatshirt while I was unconscious, so I woke up comfortable.

Despite my and Juniper's casual attire, Oliver was dressed up. He wore his usual green hat, a pair of black pants, and a t-shirt that had the design of a tuxedo on it— which, to be fair, was about as fancy as Oliver got.

"Where are we supposed to go this time to stop the problem child that is Derek?" wondered Juniper.

Man, was she gorgeous. I was so happy that I could call her my girlfriend. I'd never called her that out loud, though, for fear that she wouldn't like being addressed by the term and snap my neck. I really wanted to do something for her to let her know that I loved her. You know, something besides an uncomfortably long road trip to our impending doom.

I had heard that, supposedly, some girl from school was throwing a party, and, if I did the math right— which I usually do— it was tonight.

Speaking of school, I was actually starting to miss it. Sure, I was the type of kid to get straight D's and F's, but math was my only A. I was top of the class. I had always excelled in math, probably because everything in math is constant and has a definite answer and solution, unlike my life. I missed when my biggest problems used to be preparing for tests, which I never did anyways.

But aside from that and back to the problem at hand, before I began planning our date, I had to figure out where, and what, exactly, this new problem was, and the threats it could cause to me and my friends, family, and the lives of innocents– whether they be Shifters or any other beings.

I touched a hand to my face and felt along the side of my nose where Kyra had left scars that traveled up and across my left eye. The left side of my neck burned from where she had ripped me open and gouged her fingers into it, leaving long scars as well– a permanent reminder of that day. It still felt pretty raw, but the most concerning part was some of the numbness.

"I have no idea, but I did see a sign that said 'Welcome to Massachusetts' on it," I remembered, finally answering June's question.

"So, you *do* have an idea," said Oliver.

"Huh... I guess I do."

"But *where* in Massachusetts?" wondered Juniper.

"Quick, what's the first thing that pops into your head when you hear Massachusetts?" I asked the group.

"Food," answered Oliver.

I stared at him for a minute, contemplating what he had just said. There was no way.

"That's it? No towns or landmarks? Just food?"

"Food," repeated Oliver.

"Alrighty then. Your turn, Juniper."

"Salem," she responded.

"Exactly!" I said with a finger snap. "And I'll bet you anything that he's headed there, if he's not there already."

"You're right!" exclaimed Juniper. "It's so simple! That's where Anput is rumored to have been buried."

I snapped my fingers again. "Exactly."

"Yippee! You idiots figured it out! Now get on with it," yelled Lycan.

"Ah, ah, ah! What's the magic word?" I scolded.

"Humph," grumped Lycan. *"**Please** get on with it."*

"I would've accepted abracadabra, but that'll work too," I shrugged.

"Hey! Derek's a Shifter. Why don't we just sick Kris and the Huntsmen after him? Have the hounds tear him apart. Save us some time to do other things," suggested Oliver.

"What kinds of other things?" I prodded him.

"Oh, you know... school, homework, sleep...... dates......" muttered Oliver.

"Dates? How? I thought you were here the entire time," I said.

"The world doesn't revolve around you, Zade. It revolves around the Sun," said Oliver.

"I would've stayed if it had been you!"

"And I'm sure you would've!" said Oliver. "But I met up with Serena, sort of told her about Shifters, and then scheduled our next date."

"You WHAT? Juniper, you let this wacko into the world?" I exclaimed.

"I had no other choice! I needed him out of the place," Juniper admitted. "The nut was driving me crazy at full speed! Plus, if he didn't leave, I wouldn't be sitting here next to you."

"Why? Because I would've beaten you in a fight?" theorized Oliver.

"No," replied Juniper, "because you would be missing, and I would be in jail, crap-turd."

"It's not too late for a fight," encouraged Lycan. *"It's never too late for a fight."*

"Oliver, did you tell her about *us*?" I asked.

"Well DUH! If we're going to spend the rest of our lives together, I think it would be only fair that she knew," said Oliver.

Oh, come *on*, Oliver! You're supposed to be smart!

"*FIGHT! FIGHT! FIGHT! FIGHT!*" chanted Lycan.

I took a deep breath in, then exhaled. "Okay. Here's what's going to happen. You can go on your date tonight with Serena, and June and are gonna take a little break. Okay?"

"Okay," agreed Oliver.

"Okay...." I laid back down on the bed. Just what I needed. Oliver had told a Human about Shifters. And me. And Juniper. And the Sky Fire. And anything else that had to do with us.

"When is your date?" asked Juniper.

"Well, exactly five minutes from now," Oliver explained.

"How are you getting there?" I wondered. Oliver *still* can't drive. He's horrible at it. Just awful. Scary, even. If Oliver ever does get his license one day, I was going to have to resort to walking everywhere just to ensure he never crashes into me. On second thought, maybe walking would be worse...

"Serena is picking me up! I told her where she could find me, and I gave her directions to Ralph's cabin."

I felt a vein pop out of my forehead. I knew nothing about this Serena girl other than the fact that Oliver really liked her. For all we knew, she could belong to the Huntsmen. Or worse: belong to Derek.

I pointed out the small circular window in the attic. "Is that her?" A small red car pulled up to the cabin's door, and the driver honked the horn.

"There's my ride," smiled Oliver, climbing down the hatch. "See you losers later."

"As long as it's not a murderer pulling into the driveway, I'm good," I said.

"I'm sure Ralph's sign will do its job," laughed Juniper.

When Oliver was gone, and the car was just pulling out of the driveway, I turned my head back to Juniper, who was finally starting to relax.

"That guy." I shook my head. "I swear, he's going to be the reason I end up in a mental hospital."

"I think you'd end up there anyways," smirked Lycan.

"Ha-ha, you're soooo funny!" I rolled my eyes. "You should become a comedian. Standup's not an option, though, without your legs."

"*Please*," Lycan scoffed, "*if I became a comedian, then no one would laugh.*"

"No one is."

"*False! I can see your little girly-friend over there snickering!*"

"Can't we just skip this guy over a pond or something?" I asked.

"*Nope*," said Lycan, "*just admit it– you need me.*"

3
KYRA
Back in town

I was furious. My boyfriend told me to find Zade again, and then practically disappeared off the face of the planet. I knew what he was planning was something big.

Speaking of Zade, I had not been sleeping well ever since our fight back in Michigan.

I'd been having this reoccurring nightmare about him. The dream would start out okay, just me sitting on my bed back in my room at home. But from there, the illusion took a twisted turn. Zade would walk in, blood pouring out of the wounds I had given him across his face and neck, streaming down his skin. His head would jerk to the side occasionally, and he'd give me this unnerving, almost cartoon looking grin before repeatedly asking in a voice that sounded like two: "*What's wrong, Kyra? Why don't you love me? What's wrong with me?*"

And if that wasn't terrifying enough, he'd slowly inch closer after every time he asked those three questions until he had me cornered.

By then, I'd have worked up the courage to say something back.

"You're not welcome here!" I'd yell at the deranged apparition of my little brother. "You're a monster!"

Crazy Zade would stop dead in his tracks, blocking my path. The only thing he ever said to me after that was one little sentence.

He'd look me dead in the eyes, his now solid black eyes meeting with my brown ones, and say in the most somber voice I had heard him talk in since the beginning of the nightmare, "***You*** *turned me into this.*"

Then I'd wake up.

Man, guilt sucks.

I shook my head to snap out of the memory. I'd been sitting in my yellow car, hidden behind some trees near the forest border for over an hour, now, waiting for a sign of my brother. I knew he was too smart, or, at least his buddies were, to stay at our parents' place, but he was definitely too dumb to find a place that wasn't in Salem.

I knew he'd be at Ralph's, the man that used to babysit us both when we were kids.

Derek's plan was brilliant– taking out two birds with one stone; however, I had no idea what bird Derek was taking out with his stone. He tended to keep things to himself lately...

A red car pulled out from the driveway and onto the dirt road, pulling me away from my thoughts. I was at a comfortable distance away from the oncoming vehicle that it was far enough for whoever was inside to not notice me, but close enough so I could tell who was inside, and where they were coming from. That was just the sign I was looking for.

I watched as the car turned in the opposite direction of me, saw my chance, and turned into the forest. I pulled up next to an old log cabin with a clearly handmade sign that read: **Keep Out.**

I hated to do this, but for Derek's new and improved plan to work, I had to apologize to my brother– and it needed to sound genuine. It was a good thing I took drama class when I was still in high school, though I would much rather be helping Derek to do whatever it was that he was doing. Things with Zade were going to be awkward. I basically accused him of conspiring to kill me, then ripped his face off. Then again, he *did* light my boyfriend on fire, so maybe we're even.

Derek was counting on me. I needed to get some of his blood, and it needed to be as fresh as possible. He told me to get Zade to somehow believe that I was on his side, and if he didn't buy it, kill him, which was something I was still on the fence about. If Zade really wanted to kill me, like Derek seems to think is the case, why didn't he when he had the chance back in Michigan?

I dismissed the thought.

It shouldn't be too hard to get what Derek wants seeing as my brother should be weaker now, considering the amount of energy he had to have exerted to create the explosion that gave me a mild concussion.

Derek got the worst of it, though.

All really is fair in love and war. Except, there wasn't much of the love. It was more like the war part of the saying.

I turned my headlights off so it wouldn't be so noticeable if there were, in fact, people in the cabin.

It was time to go.

4
OLIVER
Our waiter serves us punch

I sat at a table across from Serena in Olive Garden. We had just taken our seats in the dimly lit restaurant and were already talking nonstop. Well, it was mainly Serena doing most of the talking, but I didn't mind. I was too afraid to say something stupid and ruin the entire night and add another incident to my long list of things to randomly remember and cringe about when I tried to go to sleep.

Our table was seated next to a frustrated Spanish speaking couple, who were trying to communicate with their non-Spanish speaking waiter. I overheard the woman say a phrase in her native language. I had no idea what she said, and neither did their waiter.

I focused my full attention back to our table.

Serena looked so beautiful. She was wearing a black cocktail dress with silver accessories— such as earrings, a small necklace, and a bracelet on her right wrist. She wore her usually stick straight orange-red hair in a neat, curly bun atop her head that was held together with a sparkly hair clip. She looked like she should be just about anywhere else other than an Olive Garden, but that's as fancy as I could buy right now.

Our waiter— a man with dusty blond hair wearing a black long sleeve shirt and matching slacks with a small apron tied around his waist— finally made his way over to us. "Hello, my name is Ivan, and I'll be your waiter for tonight, okay?" said the black-dressed man. He spoke with a slight accent, most likely a Ukrainian one.

"Okay," I nodded, trying hard, but failing to mock Ivan's accent.

Ivan handed me and Serena each a menu, and I couldn't help but feel something was wrong with our waiter. The way he eyed us was a little too strange.

"I shall be back to take your orders, but for now, what would you like for drink?" asked Ivan.

"Water's fine," said Serena.

I scanned my menu. "Chocolate milk, please. Oh, and if you could include a crazy straw, that would be *much* appreciated," I added. "*Much.*"

I knew by the look on Serena's face that chocolate milk was probably not the way to go for our first date, especially at a fairly decent place like Olive Garden, but I just really wanted the sweet and comforting taste of chocolate milk with the fun twist of a crazy straw. Those things are downright CRAZY!

Ivan wrote down our orders on a small notepad and walked back to the kitchen.

"Dang! I should've ordered chocolate milk, too!" Serena shook her head.

I made a mental note that Serena was awesome and should never be doubted. "Yeah, it is pretty good..." I nodded.

I felt too awkward trying to make conversation that I realized that I hadn't said anything important for a few long, grueling minutes. I had to do something about it so my first date with Serena ever didn't turn into my last date ever.

"So..." I began, breaking the silence. "What are you going to order?"

"I'm leaning towards the steak," answered Serena, still looking over the menu. "What looks good to you?"

"You do," I smiled awkwardly. Yikes! Abort mission, Oliver. Abort mission!

Serena's cheeks turned bright red, almost matching the shade of her hair.

"I–I mean the lasagna. I think I'll have the lasagna," I stuttered.

"You're as cheesy as the lasagna," joked Serena.

Great. The date had just started and already I was making a fool of myself. At this rate, I was never going to get a girlfriend. Forever unicycle.

"So......" I said. "You come here often?"

"Is that *really* how you want to start off our conversation?" asked Serena with an eyebrow as raised as her expectations that I felt I was having trouble meeting.

"No....."

"I'll help you out," she said. "Where were you a week ago? You didn't show up to school at all. Is everything all right?"

"Yeah. Me and my buds were just defending all of humanity. Just your average Friday night."

"COOL!" she exclaimed. "Does this have any relation to what you told me about Shifters?"

"Every bit of it." I was loving the spotlight. With Serena, I *finally* felt like the main character in my own life.

"Details, please!" she squealed, excitedly clapping her hands together.

"Well, long story short, my best friend turned out to be linked to dead spirits in the sky and we had to travel to Michigan to find a rude talking rock and on the way we stopped at McDonalds and he and this girl became an item and we saw Huntsmen so we left and I got scared and puked a little in my mouth and we got back on the road until we broke down so a shady burly tattooed man with a weird eye offered us a ride in his semi-truck so my friend accepted even though I disagreed with him but we went anyways and when we finished our donuts and finally arrived at a museum weird stuff happened and then we found the mean rock and got back on the road but our victory was short lived because the rock's eyes started to glow because my friends' evil older sister– long story– and her boyfriend– even longer story– drove us off of the road and the scary man with the tattoos and the convulsing eye died in friend number one's hands and he got upset and he screamed a scream of the damned and there was a fight and friend number two got hurt so number one made a fire and people blew up and when he finally woke up moons later he said we had a problem because, you know, everything has to be difficult with him, and friend number two threatened me and now I'm here," I said super fast, not pausing to take a single breath of air.

There was a small pause before Serena finally spoke. "Is it weird that I somehow followed most of that?" she asked.

"Nope. That makes things much less complicated for me."

Ivan approached our table, carrying our drinks out on a small oval tray. He set the glass of water down in front of Serena, and a plastic cup with a crazy straw sticking out of the lid in front of me. It was much appreciated.

"Here your drinks," said Ivan with his thick Ukrainian accent. "You order now?"

"I'll have the steak, medium-well, please," said Serena.

"And I would like the lasagna," I ordered.

"Okay," nodded Ivan as he wrote down the orders. "I will bring food next time I come."

Ivan retreated back into the restaurant's kitchen to prepare our food.

"In your long explanation, you mentioned there being another problem. What's the problem?" wondered Serena.

"How should I know? Ask Mr. Magic. All I do is follow him around."

"Geez... no need to get so defensive about it."

"I'm sorry..." I apologized. "I'm just getting tired of getting into trouble. I really don't know what the problem is yet, otherwise I would definitely tell you. All I know is that it has something to do with going to Salem, Massachusetts."

"Can I come?" asked Serena.

"What?" I did a double take.

"Please let me come!" pleaded Serena. "I don't wanna just hear your stories, I wanna live them! I promise I won't get in your way. I just want to help."

"Totally!" I smiled. "I mean, if you really want to, that is. Will your parents be okay with it?"

"They don't have to know. They're both on vacation in Hawaii and left the house all to myself. Something about a 'responsibility test,' but something tells me it's more of a 'get away and relax on the beach with no responsibility' thing."

"Yeah, sure!" I nodded. "You can come!"

"Yay!" cheered Serena, clapping her hands again.

Ivan our Ukrainian waiter returned to our table. *Just* Ivan. *No* food.

"Um, Ivan, where's our food?" wondered Serena.

"Yeah, what gives, man?" I complained. "You said you would bring food the next time you came out."

"How about some punch?" said Ivan.

"Wha–" I was cut off as Ivan took a swing at me, and clocked me in my face, knocking me out of my chair and onto the ground.

"That is *NOT* what I ordered!" I rubbed the side of my face where Ivan's fist collided with my head.

"I, too, have orders," said Ivan, pulling a small silver arrow from out of his apron pocket.

The non-English-speaking Spanish couple seated at the table near us began to spaz out, waving their arms in the air like they just didn't care, and yelling more Spanish words at their poor waiter.

"Dude!" exclaimed Serena. "What, do you want a tip or something?"

I took a look around the restaurant, trying to get my bearings. If Ivan said he had orders, it either came from Kris or Derek. But if it was Derek, how would he have known I would be at Olive Garden? I turned my head to the left. Far away on the other side of the restaurant, I spotted a head of ratty looking red hair. Kris. It was definitely Kris. Man, that guy was relentless! Can't a guy eat without having to run for his life? It's very hard to run fast on a full, or empty, stomach.

"Serena, we need to leave. *Now.*"

Serena stood up from the table, pushing her chair out as she did so. Ivan glared at her. She balled her fist and popped him in his nose, right between his beady little brown eyes.

Ivan was completely taken aback, and the blow to his face was enough to throw him off balance, sending him crashing into a nearby waitress carrying a tray of food. He dropped his arrow, and it landed in a bowl of hot soup. Serena kicked him just for good measure.

She extended a hand to me, offering to help me to my feet. I took her hand and stood up, dusting off my fanciest tuxedo-print shirt. "Where'd you learn to fight like that?"

"Honestly, I learned all I know about fighting from binge watching action movies on Netflix..." laughed Serena.

With all eyes on us, I grabbed her hand. "We'll, you're dang good at it! Let's get out of here."

The silver arrow whizzed by, narrowly missing my head by a hair. Rude! You can't just throw arrows at people, Ivan! Stabbing is a no-no!

"Faster, please," I urged, now dragging Serena behind me as we ran and maneuvered around tables of customers and waiters walking around.

"What *was* that guy?" exclaimed Serena.

I turned to look at her. "Ever heard of Huntsmen?"

5
JUNIPER
Cabin fever

I fiddled with the charm on Lycan's necklace that I wore around my neck and studied the random pattern of swirls engraved on the golden medallion.

Zade was standing up, looking out a circular window– the only window in Ralph's attic. Suddenly, he pointed a finger at something outside.

"Are they really back already?" he asked.

I got up and strode over to the window and took my place beside Zade to see what he was looking at. I grasped his hand tightly. He just felt right, and something was *definitely* wrong.

"Zade," I said, "that is a *yellow* car. Oliver left with Serena in a *red* car. Kyra is the only person we know who drives a highlighter."

"But how?" Zade wondered. "How does she know we're here?"

"How the heck am I supposed to know?" I shot back.

"If her car's here, where is she?" Zade wondered.

"Right here," said a familiar voice from behind us.

Zade and I whipped around and came face to face with Kyra, who was standing next to the open hatch with her arms folded across her chest. Her long, straight black hair was pulled back into a neat ponytail, and she wore a dark purple shirt with lace sleeves, matched with distressed denim skinny jeans, and a pair of black ankle-high boots to top it all off. She was in good condition despite our scuffle just a few moons ago. She'd definitely seen worse.

I quickly flung open the drawer on the nightstand that was beside the bed, and whipped out a silver knife from inside of it.

The knife was incredibly sharp, and the handle was wrapped in a brown gauze for gripping purposes. Above the handle and below the base of the blade was the head of a wolf– its eyes made out of rubies. Basically, it looked like a blade was erupting out of a wolf's head.

"Whoa!" awed Zade. "Where'd you get that?"

"Ralph's backup plan," I answered, making sure to brandish it in front of Kyra. "Just in case something like this happened, he put the knife in an easily accessible place. Used to be William's. Now, get behind me," I instructed.

I pushed Zade behind me, the knife in front, ready to strike at any moment. I so badly wanted to kill Kyra right then and there, but I knew I had to wait... at least until she was done explaining to us why– and how– she was here.

"Anger is not a good look on you, Kyra," said Zade.

"You don't look too good yourself." She focused her eyes on the claw marks across Zade's face.

That was it. That was all it took, apparently. I felt something inside of me snap, and I could no longer contain my rage. I lunged at Kyra, pinning her against the wall, holding her throat. I held the blade against Kyra's neck with my other hand.

Kyra struggled to break free of my grasp, but to no avail.

"Zade, just say the word and I'll end her pathetic life," I growled, my painted fingernails phasing and curling into long wolf claws.

"Are you really gonna let her do this to me, Zade?" said Kyra, gasping for air.

"SAY IT!" I commanded. "Give me the okay and I'll slice her throat open and gut her!"

"Zade, I'm your *sister*!" cried Kyra, her voice raspy as she tried to breathe. "You don't understand how dangerous you really are! Derek knows what to do, so you can either come with me quietly, or I will have no choice but to make sure you never hurt anyone, and you *know* what I'm implying."

"If you won't do it, I will," I threatened.

I tightened my grip on Kyra's neck, my sharp claws digging into her flesh, and inched the silver blade closer to her throat.

"NO!" Zade screamed.

"What?" I snarled.

"No," he said again. "Juniper, don't. Please." Zade's voice was quiet now, almost a whisper.

"But, Zade," I protested. "You don't seem to remember, so just let me remind you that she tried to kill you."

"June..." pushed Zade.

I let go of my grip on Kyra's throat and backed away, sheathing the knife in its matching brown leather case, and slid it into my belt loop. I retracted my claws as well. I had the guts Zade didn't.

Kyra slid down the wall and curled up into a ball on the floor, gasping for breath.

Zade started for Kyra to help her up, but I blocked him with an arm, stopping him from going any further. "Don't."

Zade hung his head, but did nothing to get around me.

"You know very well that there is no way I am letting you go with her, so grab my phone," I told him, grabbing the Lycan Stone and shoving it into Zade's blue and gray backpack.

He picked up my phone from the rocking chair. "Got it."

"Great." I climbed down the ladder of the hatch with his backpack slung across my shoulder. "Follow me."

6
ZADE

Juniper can drive a motorcycle.

Who knew?

I followed Juniper out of Ralph's cabin, into the driveway and straight towards an old, rusted Harley-Davidson motorcycle.

It was dark out, but the distant lights of the city made the trees seem to light up. It was peaceful and quiet out, and the only sound I heard was the faint chirping of crickets, distant sounds of cars on the main road, and me and Juniper's footsteps on the cement driveway.

"Get on," she instructed, handing me my backpack and then strapping a black helmet to her head.

I did the same as she and strapped the matching helmet on as well, which really clashed with my green

Ducks sweatshirt. I put my backpack on both of my shoulders to ensure a safe ride. I loved that backpack. Backpack is good. Backpack is life.

"What are we doing?" I asked. "I don't know how to drive a motorcycle."

"Who said anything about *you* driving?" smirked Juniper.

"Do you even know how to drive a motorcycle?"

"DUH! Of course I do!" Juniper answered, climbing onto the bike. "What, you mean to tell me you *can't?*"

"Well... no."

"Just get on," she sighed. "We're going to find another place to go for the time being. Get Kyra off our trail. Then, if all goes well, we can come back here. She won't look here again if she thinks we left for good."

"I know where we could go!" I said, carefully climbing onto the back of the motorcycle. "There's a party at Robyn's house tonight... I thought that maybe you and I could go back before any of this happened. It'd been buzzing around for a while since she found out her parents would be out of town tonight. This seems like a good excuse."

"Robyn? Robyn Abbot? That emo kid who sits in the back of my French class? She's rude."

"As rude as you?" I raised an eyebrow.

"Touché," shrugged Juniper. "Fine. Why not. It'll be the last place Kyra would look for us, if she can even recover. Text Oliver and let him know where to go so he won't end up as Kyra chow."

I whipped out Juniper's phone from inside my pants pocket and scrolled through her contacts.

"Okay, so I'm looking in the 'O' section, and he's not listed. Did you delete his number or something?" I asked.

"Oh, he's not under 'O,'" stated Juniper with a sly grin spreading across her face.

"Where is he then?"

"I have him listed under 'T' for 'Train wreck.'"

Yep. Found him.

She lifted the bike's kickstand and started the engine, which took a couple of tries since the vehicle was so old. Then, when we were all situated and the message to Oliver was sent, she pulled out of the driveway and onto the gravel road that would take us into town, far away from Kyra.

7
ZADE
We crash a party and I can't stop making puns

I never thought I would ever be on a motorcycle. It was just something I never saw myself doing; that is, until now. Who would've guessed that Ralph had a motorcycle, and Juniper knew how to drive it?

Well, Juniper knowing how to drive a motorcycle wasn't very surprising. She could do a lot of things.

For example; she knew how to make homemade potato chips, which, by the way, was the best thing I had ever had EVER. We used to eat so much of that snack whenever we would have our '*hangout dates.*' And she also knew how to pick various locks using nothing but a bobby pin and lip-gloss. She was good at that sort of stuff, problem solving. She always had a solution for anything, always analyzing things, which was a necessary skill for her to have beings she wanted to be a detective once she got into the real world. Her dad was actually a police officer, so her growing up with him and his way of thinking has had its advantages. She'd be her own K-9 unit, though I would never actually tell her that to her face. She'd probably rip off the other half of it.

But just thinking about Ralph on a motorcycle cracked me up. His beard probably flew around in his face. That would be hilarious to watch, although, something told me that this old motorcycle was William's.

I clung to Juniper's side tighter. I did NOT want to end up like the roadkill we saw a couple miles back. Plus, she smelled good. But that poor, unfortunate squirrel was probably just looking for some acorns and decided follow the chicken's lead to cross the road, and then BAM! Oops, that was a car....

Despite the squirrel's death, I was still excited to go to that party with Juniper. It was probably our last chance to pretend like things were normal, like they used to be before I knew I was a one-man screamo band, and all that stupid moon crap.

"Hey, June," I said, "the funny thing about us riding this motorcycle is that it's appropriate to say it's a '*Vroom*' stick!"

"Zade," sighed Juniper, "I thought we were past the puns."

"Never!" I exclaimed. "Pun fun forever!"

The city lights grew brighter as we neared the brightly lit street where, at the very end of the block, Robyn's house was located. Juniper pulled over to the edge of the curb and parked the motorcycle.

She climbed off the bike, unlike me, who accidentally slid off the leather seat and landed flat on my back on the sidewalk.

"You see? It's a good thing I was wearing a helmet," I said.

"Yeah, wouldn't wanna damage what you barely have there," smiled Juniper as she unclipped her helmet and removed it from her head, dangling it on the motorcycle's handlebar.

I stood up, my helmet already off, and set it on the seat. "OH NOOOOO!" I screamed, bending back down to the ground and cradling a small dead bug in my hands. "I killed it!"

"Calm down, buddy," said Juniper, sarcastically patting me on the back. She had no empathy.

"If only I had lightning powers!" I sobbed, still talking to the deceased insect. "I'm sorry, all I can do is cremate you."

I gently set the bug down in the grass and stood back up.

"Are you finished?" she said.

I nodded. "Well, are you ready to be party animals?" I grinned.

"Really?" sighed Juniper. "You just had to throw that one in? That was cheap, and you know it."

"You know you like it."

Juniper just rolled her eyes and turned to the house, but she was smiling, so at least I didn't chase her off with my crappy sense of humor just yet!

I caught back up with her, and we walked up the driveway together.

8
ZADE
I'm Batman

We stood in the doorway of Robyn's huge mansion at the end of the street. Even though we were outside of the party, we could still hear the music and see the flashing lights through the windows.

Juniper knocked on the door, and after what seemed like five minutes of waiting, a girl finally opened it.

She had choppy, scene styled brown hair with long side bangs that completely covered her right eye. Her makeup-covered hazel eyes seemed to see straight through me and into my soul, just like a cat. She wore tight, ripped skinny jeans, a black tank top with some band name on it that I was probably not cool enough to listen to, black biker boots, and a green army jacket. She also sported black snake-bite piercings on her bottom lip. Edgy.

"More partiers, eh? Come on in," invited soul-sucking cat-eyes, motioning for us to follow her inside.

The inside of Robyn's house was huge. There was a grand entrance, complete with a massive marble stairway. The booming sound of the music was almost deafening, and the multi-colored flashing strobe lights further disoriented our already overwhelmed systems.

I turned to Juniper and whispered, "I think I'm gonna puke."

"You're the one who wanted to be here," she said. "Here, just hold my hand, okay?"

"I would love to, but I'm not entirely sure which one of you is the real you..." I explained.

"Really, Zade? Double vision already?"

I nodded and Juniper reached out and grabbed my hand. "Better?" she asked.

"Yeah," I smiled at Juniper.

Behind her, crazed teenagers could be seen running around rampant, screaming and trying to see how far they could throw each other.

One unfortunate guy was picked up and thrown into the huge flat screen TV in the family room.

"HEY!" cat-eyes screeched. "No wrecking the TV, you bottom feeder! Anyways," she said, redirecting her attention back to June and I, "the name's Robyn."

"And I'm Batman," I said, smiling.

"Really? 'Cause you look more like a Two-Face to me." Robyn glared at me, her soul-sucking hazel eyes still staring right through me.

"Okay, okay, my name's Zade."

"Whoa, dude," gawked Robyn while she grabbed my right arm, pulled up my sleeve, and examined my black marking, "Nice ink. You know, I'm going to get a tattoo when I turn eighteen. I'd get one sooner, but my parents won't let me, ya know? They think it's just a phase. Well, news flash, Mom and Dad, it's not just a phase!"

"Well, it's actually more of a birthmark than a tattoo..." I corrected her, yanking back my arm.

"Whatever you say, bro," Robyn shrugged, "but I've never seen a birthmark like that before. So, who are you guys anyways?"

"You wanna know how I got these *scars*?" I interrupted, pointing to the many claw-shaped disfigurements that ran across my face and neck, doing my best attempt at a pirate voice.

"No, not really..." refused Robyn.

"Just ignore my boyfriend, he's... challenged," said Juniper. "My name's Juniper."

Forget the insult, she just referred to me as her boyfriend for the first time ever!

"You guys seem cool," nodded Robyn, scanning the two of us, though I had a feeling she only meant Juniper. "You can stay. Welcome to my party. Punch is over there, bathroom there, oh! And don't break anything. If you breaky-breaky, you no wakey-wakey, got it?"

I nodded.

"All right! Have fun!

June and I stepped deeper into the house, and Robyn dispersed from us to join a group of rowdy kids who were playing a game that didn't look entirely legal.

"All right, Zade," said Juniper, still gripping my hand tight and pulling me to the side next to a long table with a pink tablecloth on it where the punch was. "I don't like it here, it's way too much for a Shifter, so this trip is going to have some purpose. We're going to do a little investigating tonight. I heard that Robyn was actually related to Mimics."

"No way," I shook my head. "They have better sense than to live around Shifters, and Salem has a pretty large Shifter population."

"Just saying what I heard," she said with a shrug.

"You really think so?"

"Not necessarily," said Juniper. "Maybe it's a small amount and the gene just got lost somewhere along the lines. Or maybe the gene was just *forgotten*. We always talk about having a balance between man and wolf. Mimics can't be that different– they shift too, just into other people. They walk the line between appearances. Maybe she just tipped the scales more to the Human side and forgot about her face-stealing ways. It is possible..."

"But–"

"Or maybe she has us all fooled," she continued, talking over me.

"Well, actually, I thought tonight could be a chance for us to–"

"I think I know where we can start. Perhaps they have some telling info somewhere.... This huge house has a ton of floors, so maybe they keep files and photos in the basement..." Juniper interrupted, thinking aloud to herself.

"Fine," I sighed, picking up a punch-filled cup and preparing to drink it.

"I wouldn't advise drinking that," warned Juniper. "There's a lot of delinquents around here. You don't know what horrors could be in that single cup of punch."

"I bet it's fine. You have to give people a chance, June."

"All right," surrendered Juniper, "but it's your funeral."

I raised the plastic cup to my lips and took a sip, then immediately spit it out. "I have some regrets," I whined.

"I told you," Juniper smiled.

"Oh, it burns!" My tongue hung out of my mouth as I repeatedly wiped my hands on it, trying to get rid of the awful taste.

"I told you not to drink the punch, but you did it anyways. On the bright side, I finally have a nickname for you, Spike," she winked.

"Oh, ha-ha-ha."

"I'm going to check out the basement. Please stay here and try not to die. I know that's hard for you."

"No way!" I protested. "You are *not* leaving me here alone with all these crazies! If you go anywhere, I'm coming with."

"Good, cause I really didn't want to be left alone. I mean, I am perfectly capable of defending myself, don't get me wrong, but I feel more comfortable when you're with me... for your own sake."

Juniper and I started for the stairway, but stopped in our tracks when we heard the front door that we came in through creak open, then slam shut.

"Who do you think that was?" I asked her.

"No idea," said Juniper, "but whoever it was had better not be looking for us."

9
SERENA
Friends in low places

We were looking for Zade and Juniper.

I stepped into the huge mansion of a house, trailed by Oliver, who assured me that this was the right place. I wasn't sure about that. No offense to Oliver, but this didn't look like his scene.

I wasn't too happy about going to some girl I'd never met before's party, but, according to Oliver, his friends had told him to meet up with them here, which seemed kinda strange, because Oliver *really* didn't strike me as the party type, never mind be friends with some.

I was still excited to meet them, though. From what Oliver told me, they seemed like some pretty *interesting* characters.

"Hey, Z-dude!" Oliver grabbed my hand and drug me through the massive crowd of partiers in the direction of a couple.

The guy had tousled, short and wavy jet-black hair that suited his tan complexion, with long, painful looking scars carved into his slim, angular face that also ran down his neck, which was a bit of a red flag to me. He was apparently a fan of the Ducks, if the green hoodie he was wearing was anything to go off of. The most random thing about him was the backpack slung across his right shoulder. That must've been the Zade Oliver told me about.

The girl next to Zade was a major contrast in comparison to him in both the colors of her characteristics and the shape of her features, which were much less angular than his, and unlike me, she was tall and had a model body type— long, lean and thin— whereas I was shorter and curvier. She had curly blond hair and looked pretty intimidating with her shapely, thinly trimmed eyebrows arching over deep-set, light green eyes glaring in me and Oliver's direction. I guessed that she was Juniper, Oliver's other friend that was always picking on him. She looked mean.

Oliver slowed to a stop, causing me to bump into him. He let go of my hand and began to do a long and complicated handshake with Zade while Juniper stood in the back and glared daggers at Oliver. I was sure she was about to burn a hole through his skull any second now.

After the ridiculously long handshake performed by the two was over, Zade focused his dark puppy dog eyes on me.

I immediately felt small. His gaze was holding and intimidating, but despite the panic he instilled in me, there was something calming about him. He was a good-looking guy, but personally, I preferred Oliver. This Zade guy gave off a vibe that was a little wild and impulsive, while Oliver was a little more thoughtful and sweet.

Even Zade's appearance was more in-your-face than Oliver's. He had sharper, more angular features and darker color tones, whereas Oliver was the opposite, and was just overall softer.

"You must be Serena," he said, confirming that I was in fact right about who these people were. "I'm Zade." He outstretched his right arm to shake my hand. I noticed there was a black marking on his wrist poking out of his sweater sleeve. Oliver had told me before that this was because of him being what they called the 'Zenith.' It sounded a little crazy, but I didn't doubt it. I had always been a big believer in the supernatural.

Having been raised in Alaska for the majority of my childhood I had heard many folklore and legends, and to me, these... *creatures...* were no different. If they were real, who knew what else was out there.

Juniper approached me and looked me over. "Hmmmm...." she hummed, rubbing her chin. "You must have some psychological problems to want to go on a date with Oliver."

"Nope," I shook my head, "I'm psycho-free!"

"Okay..." Juniper said, still eyeing me suspiciously.

"C'mon, June, give the girl a break," said Zade.

"It's fine," I said. I instinctively reached for my pocket, which I didn't have. Dang dress! I wanted my lucky dog whistle. Yes, I'm superstitious, and no, I don't care if it's stupid. I guess it's in my purse, which I left in the car. I bet if I'd brought it with, our date would have been smoother.

"You two got here surprisingly fast for a last-minute change on date night," said Zade.

"Well, it wasn't too hard to get away when your waiter is from the U-*cray*-ne," Oliver joked. "He turned on us faster than a tuna salad left in the midsummer heat for an hour. He was a Huntsman, so we had no problem bashing his face in in front of a crowd."

"Yeah," I giggled. "*We.*"

"So..." started Oliver, "It must've been a real emergency for Juniper not to insult me in her text message."

"Actually, I sent that message," said Zade.

"Oh... so that's why my ego didn't get a hole blown into it that time," Oliver said. "And to think I was starting to get pretty worried about you."

"Don't get used to it, you halfwit ignoramus, that was a one-time thing," warned Juniper.

"I walked right into that one."

"More like waltzed right into that one, buddy," said Zade.

"So, what really happened that you told us not to come back to Ralph's?" asked Oliver.

"Well, Sir Stupid, Kyra showed up and tried to off us," Juniper revealed.

"WHAT?" exclaimed Oliver. "What happened? How did she find you, and what did you do?"

"I have no idea how she found us, but if you'd clean the lint out of your ears, you would've already heard me say that she tried to kill us. So, I did what any rational person would've done. I pulled a knife up to her neck and held her up against a wall, threatening to kill her," said a perky Juniper.

"It's going to be an interesting Thanksgiving," kidded Zade.

Okay, now I was lost. "Sorry to interrupt," I apologized, "but I am *not* following a thing you guys are saying."

"*Basically, Zade here's sissy-poo wants him to give himself up so she can have a relationship with her power-hungry boyfriend*," said a muffled voice from inside Zade's backpack. Wow, it just gets weirder and weirder.

"Lycan," Zade, Oliver, and Juniper all groaned in unison.

"I completely forgot about the guy," admitted Zade.

"Oh no!" Juniper gasped. "Speaking of completely forgetting about things: Ralph."

"WHAT!" exclaimed Oliver.

"He'll be fine. I mean, we left Kyra pretty winded, and Ralph's a strong guy," said Zade. "Plus, Ralph's in town. Kyra should be gone by the time he gets back."

"Ralph's old, Zade, and he doesn't even know what's going on. Sooner or later, they'll cross paths," said a concerned Oliver.

"I'm sorry," I interrupted again, "but who is '*Ralph?*'"

"A very important Shifter," Oliver explained.

"Who also happens to be a trusted family friend, Council member, and my godfather," added Zade.

Juniper nervously fiddled with the golden swirl pendant dangling from the gold chain necklace hanging from her neck.

"*You idiots really messed up now!*" laughed Lycan.

"Shut up, Lycan!" scolded Zade. "People are going to think I'm crazy, talking to a backpack."

"*What, like they didn't before?*"

"*What, like they didn't before?*" mocked Zade in a high-pitched voice.

"First of all," started Juniper, "Zade, you said you didn't want to talk to your backpack, so stop talking to your backpack."

"*HA!*" laughed Lycan from inside Zade's bag.

"And Lycan," said Juniper, "you're a murderer. Shut up."

"*I just love our little talks,*" Lycan sassed.

"Listen, Ralph will be fine," consoled Juniper. "Unless one of you have his number, or if Ralph even has a phone to begin with, we can't do anything about it. We have to find an explanation for Zade's dream-vision-thingy, and I think we can find an answer somewhere in this house."

"Dream-vision-thingy?" I repeated, confused.

"I'm psyched," said Zade.

"Psychic," corrected Juniper.

"I'm psychic."

"Not really. He's really not," objected Juniper, shaking her head.

"I just occasionally *see* things. In my head. While I'm asleep. That translate into real life when I'm awake. About death."

"And moons!" added Oliver.

"Yes, and moons!" Zade agreed.

"Oh. Okay," I nodded, slightly weirded out.

I was seriously starting to question why I even talked to a guy wearing a taco shirt in the first place. They all seemed like wackadoos. Shifters, fire in the sky, and an evil ginger with a love for archery? Seriously? Oh, and don't forget the pyromaniac's crazy older sister and her boyfriend who apparently attempted to murder them all last week! I was growing more and more skeptical after every word that came out of their shifty mouths. But, despite my better judgement, I had a gut feeling that I was meant to meet these people, and my gut *never* steered me wrong.

"I can tell you're not buying all of this," said Zade, "So, I'm gonna show you some proof. You want some proof?" Zade thrust his hand out in front of me, his nails now long, curled, sharp, and inhuman. They were wolf claws. "There's your proof."

"Wha... whoa..." I struggled to say. I pricked the tip of my finger on one of Zade's claws. "Those... those are *real*. Like, *really real*."

"Listen," said Juniper, "I know this may be a lot to take in, but what we're telling you is the truth. So, are you with us, or are you against us?"

"I'm…" I started. This was my chance to get out of this madness while I still had a chance, but something in me didn't want to. "I'm with you."

"Good. Otherwise I would have to kill you," smiled Juniper. "Any who, we found out that Robyn could quite possibly be related to Mimics. Mimics are what killed Anput. That's our mystery for tonight. Zade and I will check downstairs for clues as to what is going on in Zade's vision, and Oliver and you can look for anything that seems suspicious or relevant up here."

"Aye-aye, captain," said Oliver, and our group split up.

10
DEREK
I'm the moon's auto-correct

I had the perfect plan-B. Well, it wasn't really a '*plan-B,*' but more so of a part two, try-again-but-this-time-smarter kind of thing.

All I needed was the next two moons to pass by quickly so that October thirty-first, the night of the blue moon, would be here, and the coin, which Kyra has, would be returned to me.

July was the last predicted blue moon for a long time, and July came and went before I had the means to perform what I was attempting now. I planned to use it to my advantage.

Zade was the Zenith, and nothing I could do would ever change that— that is, unless I did this. It was no longer a necessity to kill Zade, either. It's impossible to take the Zeniths' power the hard way. I still had a knot on the back of my head from the blast to prove it. But it would still be nice to get Zade out of the way so there would be no interference. Killing him was optional, but it would be a wonderful luxury. Besides, things needed to get a little messy for part two to work.

That's why I sent Kyra back to Oregon while I went to Massachusetts. That way I didn't have to get my hands dirty and would be ready when the time came. I'd been preparing for this moment my entire life, and this time it would yield results. But since Kyra had yet to return with a vial of his blood and the coin she refuses to let out of her sight, I couldn't do anything but sit in my hotel room and wait.

I knew I was doing the right thing, even if no one else thought the same. Zade is too young and unpredictable, and I know that if he gets too aggressive, he could do some real damage. That's why I want him dead in the first place. I would finally show my father what I was capable of– who I was really meant to be.

I laughed.

It was stupid, the things we would fight about, just because my mother died in childbirth. The fighting got physical, even. That's why I had to jump at this chance. I'd finally make him understand.

The only part I wasn't sure about was what to do with Kyra. There can only be one Zenith. After she delivered the coin and Zade's blood, our mission would be complete. The world would be right again.

When we finally correct Anput's wrong, I'd need her safe and out of the way. I needed her somewhere where nothing could ever harm her, and I knew just the place.

11
ZADE
I really really really really really really hate the dark

I followed Juniper's lead down the stairs and into the pitch-dark basement of Robyn's house.

I was incredibly afraid of the dark. It freaked me out so much to not be able to see my surroundings. So much, that if I was in pure darkness for over ten minutes, I had panic attacks. I knew it was strange for me, the Zenith, the fire guy connected to dead spirits, to be scared of the dark. But I was.

Juniper reached the end of the last stair and began the search for a light switch.

"Hey, June, how 'bout you look, and I'll stay right here on the stairs in case anybody shows up," I suggested.

"Yeah," laughed Juniper, "No. There is no way that is happening." She grabbed my backpack from off my shoulder, and I watched as it disappeared along with her arm into the dark.

"Packy!" I cried.

"Relax, Dora the Explorer, it's right here. But you have to come get it."

I slowly stepped off the last step, clinging to the walls beside me. "Juniper, find me. I can't see you. I'm BLIND! I'M BLIIIIIIIND! FIND ME NOW, PLEASE!"

"Zade, you dimwit, you have fire you can create in the palm of your hand. Use that as your light source," Juniper said.

"Well, I would if I knew how to do it without literally raising the roof, if you know what I mean," I explained.

"It's a good thing you're pretty," sighed Juniper.

I felt around with arms outstretched in front of me like feelers until I touched what felt like a shoulder. I shrieked, and something kneed me in the stomach, making me crumple to the ground.

"Please don't eat me, Boogeyman! I swear, my girlfriend tastes much better than I do! She eats healthier!"

"Zade!" scolded Juniper. She pulled down on a string attached to a single lightbulb dangling from the ceiling, illuminating the small room in a dim yellow glow. "Calm down, it's just me!"

"Oh. Okay. I'm okay." My heavy breathing slowed as I began to calm down.

"You'd sell me out to a monster whose name implies boogers?" said Juniper.

"You'd knee me in the gut?" I retorted.

"You screamed and it startled me. Plus, you were pretty loud, and if we get caught down here, we'll be in big trouble."

"Don't you think it's a little weird how we find all our information in peoples' basements?" I wondered.

"Yes, but we don't have time to reflect on how strange our lives are. Now, help me find something Changer-ish," Juniper instructed.

I stood up from the floor. "Hey," I said, "What's that?"

Juniper followed me to a small wooden side-table near a gray couch where a large book with a leather covering was.

I picked up the book and blew the dust off of it. "What is it?" I asked. Whatever it was, it hadn't been touched in years.

"Give it to me," said Juniper, tearing the book from my grasp. She flipped through a couple of pages which were yellow and brittle with age. "It appears to be some sort of a scrapbook," said Juniper.

"OOH! I wanna see!" I peered at the scrapbook from over her shoulder. "Hey," I said, pointing a finger at a picture of one side of a golden coin with a wolf head engraved on it, stopping Juniper from turning the page, "Isn't that the coin my dad gave Kyra when she became alpha?"

"Yeah," said Juniper, "it even says here: *The Coin of the Alphas*."

"Okay.... So why do Mimics have something like this?"

"That coin gets around. The coin is given to the alpha of the pack that the Zenith belongs to, you know, for safekeeping and stuff. It's rumored to have been made with Anput's blood, which, if you know anything about Anput, Mimics are her least favorite thing," Juniper explained. "The Council meets with other subspecies a lot. I imagine theft is a common occurrence."

"Look," I said, pointing to some wording. "It says here that 'If what is needed is gone, use blue moon and blood.'"

"I think it means that it's a backup plan in case something goes wrong. Did you see anything like this in your, um, dream?" Juniper asked.

"June, I don't remember much anymore, but what I do know for sure is that we need to get to Massachusetts, and the sooner, the better."

12
OLIVER
I don't like this, as usual

I held Serena's hand as we waded through the crowd of partiers. Juniper had told us to find something that could pass as a clue. So far, the only thing weird we'd seen was a kid trying to throw another guy to see how aerodynamic he was.

I heard my name being called and was startled to see Zade and Juniper standing behind us when I turned around.

"Oliver," repeated Zade once more, "We found something." He handed me a heavy scrapbook with a leather casing.

"What's this?" asked Serena.

"Oh, just a little something that has a certain little coin in it."

"The COTA?" I said, examining the strange thing. "Why would that be in a book like this? For Mimics, no less."

"The what?" puzzled Serena.

"COTA: Coin of the Alphas," I explained to her.

"'*Of*' and '*the*' shouldn't be included," said Juniper.

"Yeah, but COTA sounds a whole lot cooler than CA," I argued, "Otherwise you just sound like a bird." I shuddered. "Birds are mean. Why do you think there are signs like that in the park?"

"Back to the point," said Zade. "The coin is some kind of shortcut."

"What do you mean?" wondered Serena.

"Oh, I know what you're talking about! Sort of..." I said. "There was some old Shifter myth about the COTA, but I don't actually know it. The Council prevented the old tale from being passed on. I never got to hear the actual story, though. Something about a dark Zenith– like a last resort kind of deal. But it's just a myth."

"Oliver," said Juniper, "we are creatures of myth. Since when does a little story have no relevance to actual life?"

"Touché."

"The black haze I saw in my vision," recalled Zade, "must have something to do with the coin. Whatever it is it does, if it gets into the wrong hands at the wrong time..."

"There will be an unbalance," determined Juniper.

"Where are the Ancients when you need them?" said Zade.

"What do you mean by '*at the wrong time?*'" I asked.

"I don't know for sure, but I think it has something to do with the upcoming blue moon," Zade concluded.

I was not liking where this conversation was headed, but I knew there was no shortcut to fixing what was going on.

Juniper handed Zade back the scrapbook. "Keep it. You never know when a little information might help us."

"When do we leave?" I asked.

"We'll take off from the party, then we'll grab some stuff from our houses. Serena probably wants to change out of... *that*, and I have one very important stop we'll save for last," said Zade in the midst of stuffing the scrapbook into his backpack.

"Do you think Kyra still has the coin?" asked Juniper.

"It's hard to tell," said Zade. "My best guess is that it's with Derek. If not, it'll work its way to him. Kyra's long gone by now."

I knew the real reason why Zade didn't want to go back to the cabin. He didn't want to risk another possible confrontation with his sister. But Zade was right. If his dream was set in Massachusetts, then that's where we should be going. Besides, if the blue moon really did affect whatever it was that was happening, we had no time to waste.

"Are we in for a ride?" I wondered, almost afraid to hear the answer to my own question.

"Oh, always," smiled Zade.

13
SERENA
Zade sets a broom on fire

Well, I decided to trust the three crazies, and was now in the back of my car next to Oliver, with Juniper up front in the passenger's seat and Zade driving, which was probably not the best idea I'd had all day.

We did end up stopping back at the old cabin, but that Kyra girl was gone. No car or nothing. The guy named Ralph wasn't back either, apparently. The place was eerily still, and all the lights were off.

Instead of stopping at both Oliver and Juniper's houses, Oliver decided that since Zade always carried his beloved backpack full of stuff with him everywhere since their last trip, he would be just fine, and that they could save themselves another trip and just stop at Juniper's place.

That chick would not take no for an answer. There was absolutely no way Juniper was going to leave the state unprepared and without stopping at her place first. Not a chance.

As we pulled into the driveway of her big house, I couldn't shake the nagging suspicion that something wasn't quite right. Not necessarily here, but somewhere else. Something felt off.

I decided to put the weird feelings behind me and stepped out of the car and followed the three friends into Juniper's mansion of a house.

The inside looked even bigger than the outside, if that was even possible. The walls were all painted warm colors, and there was a massive leather couch in front of a flat screen TV hanging above the mantle of a fireplace in the huge living area.

"Mom?" called Juniper, "Mom, are you home?"

Suddenly a little blond head popped up from behind the leather couch. "Junie?" said a quiet voice coming from the head.

"Eric!" smiled Juniper as she rushed over to give her little brother a hug. "Is Mom around?"

"Yeah, she's in the kitchen. You were gone for a long time, Junie. Where were you?" asked Eric.

"Fighting bad guys with these two knuckleheads," she said, pointing behind her with both of her thumbs in the direction of Zade and Oliver.

"He's scary," said Eric, pointing a finger at Zade.

"I'm scary?" said Zade as he walked over to Eric and crouched down to his height. "How am I scary?"

Eric motioned for Juniper to bend over and whispered something in her ear. "Ah," she nodded, standing up, "he said you have scary eyes."

"I do not," disputed Zade.

Eric nodded.

"They're just blue, like yours," stated Zade.

"My mommy says that I have eyes that are as pretty as the sky," said Eric.

"Well," stated Zade, "my mommy always compared mine to the deep blue hue the sky turns just before moonrise, but I think they look more like the tears of my enemies," he grinned.

Eric ran away and into the kitchen with tears streaming down his face, crying "MOOOOOOOOOMMMMYYYYYYY!"

"Zade, you are not going to make him like you when you tell him stuff like that," Juniper chided.

"I can't help it. It's just the effect I have on kids," defended Zade.

Juniper shook her head.

I should've probably taken the whole 'tears of my enemies' thing as another red flag, but I was genuinely intrigued by this bunch of whack-jobs, and wanted to see what would happen next. They're sort of like a car crash; I wanna look away, but I just can't help but watch.

A woman, probably in her late forties or early fifties, stepped out of the doorway of the kitchen and into the living room wearing a white apron. Her auburn colored hair was held in place out of her face full of freckles that dusted over the bridge of her thin nose and under her amber colored eyes by a brown clip on the back of her head. "Juniper?" she said.

"Mom!" beamed Juniper, rushing towards the lady to embrace her in a bear hug.

"Oh, you brought that...... *thing*... with you, too," she said disgusted, pointing at Zade. "Oh my gosh, it's in the house. Eric, get the broom."

"It's nice to see you, too, Georgia," snarked Zade.

"Uck, don't even talk to me. And to you, I am Ms. Martin," said Georgia.

"You say that like you expect me to actually care about what comes out of your mouth," Zade snarled.

"You little punk," Georgia sneered.

"All right," interrupted Juniper, "that's enough."

"But, Juniper," protested Ms. Georgia Martin, "That boy is nothing but trouble, and is no good for you. You could end up *killed* following this doofus around!"

Juniper pulled the bottom of her shirt down a little farther.

"What was that for?"

"Nothing," said Juniper.

"Juniper Susannah Martin, what are you hiding?" pushed Georgia.

"Mom, I swear, it's nothing."

Georgia lifted the bottom of Juniper's shirt up, revealing a scar that ran from the middle of her back all the way to the right side of her lower stomach which, although completely healed over, judging by her slight wince, seemed like it still caused her great pain.

Her mother gritted her teeth.

"Mom, it wasn't his fault!" Juniper insisted.

Georgia grabbed the broomstick from a corner in the kitchen and ran after Zade, chasing and hitting him repeatedly on the head with the bristles.

Zade ran around the room like a chicken with its head cut off, jumping on and off the couch trying to escape the wrath of his girlfriend's mom and her broom.

I could tell that this was definitely one of those car crash moments.

I watched as Zade's fist erupted into a ball of blue flames. He grabbed for the bristles of the broom, lighting it on fire.

"WITCHCRAFT!" I screamed.

Georgia flailed around, screaming, as she shook the broomstick up and down, trying to put out the blue fire that was burning up the broom.

When she was finally able to put out the fire and the flames died out, all that was left was a part of the stick. Georgia took a swing at Zade, making contact with him in his lower jaw and knocking him from off the couch onto the floor. She hoisted it up as if to take another swing, but Juniper grabbed the other end and yanked it out of her mother's grasp before she got the chance to.

"Mom, it wasn't his fault. He saved me. If it wasn't for him, I wouldn't be here," Juniper explained.

Zade sat up slowly, rubbing his sore jaw and groaning.

Georgia reclaimed her stick from her daughter and walked around to the other side of the couch where Zade was and whacked him in the gut, knocking the wind out of him and causing him to double over in pain.

"MOM!" exclaimed Juniper.

"Just making sure, sweetie," smiled Georgia.

14
ZADE
Serena has a gut feeling

Juniper, Oliver, Serena, and I were all upstairs in Juniper's room. She was busy digging through her closet, searching for the perfect outfits to bring for when we took off for Massachusetts.

Oliver seemed relaxed, and was laying across Juniper's bed playing a Gameboy that he found on one of her shelves. Serena seemed a little more on edge, though, and was pacing around the room. When she would occasionally sit down, she would fidget. I couldn't really blame her, either. I was standing at Juniper's window, looking down from the second story. Something just felt...... off.

"You feel it, too?" asked Serena as she joined me at the windowsill.

"Huh?" I said, coming back into reality. "Oh, yeah, but I'm not too worried right now. Lycan's eyes aren't glowing red, so we're fine."

Serena seemed a little more nervous around me, a little more cautious, since the whole 'setting fire to the broomstick' thing happened.

"Yeah..." Serena trailed off. "So, um, about that... What even *is* that?" she asked, pointing at the bedside table where the Lycan Stone was sitting.

"*What are you lookin' at?*" challenged Lycan.

"Sassy."

"*What did you just call me, Miss Pansy?*"

"Sassy?" repeated Serena, now slightly terrified.

"*You're so lucky I don't have arms, or I would use them to strangle you!*" threatened Lycan.

"I'm sorry," apologized Serena.

"*NO! I don't accept your apology! Does this look like the face of mercy to you? HUH? DOES IT?*" screamed Lycan.

"Just ignore him and maybe he'll go away," I suggested.

"*I wish DEATH upon you, Zade!*"

"*That* is the Lycan Stone," I introduced. "I really wish we could skip him across a lake and laugh maniacally as we watch him sink to the bottom, never to resurface again, but, unfortunately, we sort of need him."

"Oh, now I remember! That's the guy that was yelling at you from inside your backpack!" recalled Serena.

"It's one of his many talents," I said.

"And the other talents are..."

"Being a jerk without a body."

"*Yes, and...*" Lycan pushed.

"Murder," I finished.

"Thank you!"

"Moving on," I turned my back to Lycan, "You're serious about coming with us to Salem?" I said, gazing out the window again.

"Why not? It sounds like an adventure, and I like to think of myself as the adventurous type," said Serena.

"There'll be danger," I warned.

"Good!" smiled Serena. "Now I'll finally have something to talk about at the dinner table when my parents get back!"

I laughed. "You're great. All right, if you really wanna come that bad, I won't stand in your way."

"Awesome!" she squealed.

"Don't get too excited. You really didn't have much of a choice. We were going to have to keep an eye on you anyways because Oliver couldn't keep his trap shut, and we wouldn't want anyone else to find out about us. Now, Serena, you wouldn't do that to us, would you?"

"N-no, sir," she stuttered.

"Good. Trust is very important to me– to all of us. Can we trust you, Serena?" I asked her. I love terrifying people like that. The scars sucked, but really helped!

"Yes," she nodded. "Yes, you can trust me."

Juniper's sing-song voice cut our conversation short. "Oooh, Serena!" she called from inside her ginormous closet. "Come here!"

"Gotta go," said Serena as she walked away and into the closet void.

I continued to gaze out the window at the starry sky. Something bad was definitely happening, there was no doubt about it.

I turned around to face Oliver, whose entire upper body was hanging off the side of Juniper's bed as he played his game.

"Suit up!" I told the gang.

"What!" Oliver sat up. "Why? I'm comfortable here. Besides, can't we just go to Massachusetts tomorrow morning, you know, when it's not pitch-black outside? Why do we have to leave *now*?" he wondered.

"We're going to make that special stop right now," I explained.

Juniper and Serena finally emerged out of Juniper's big closet full of apparel– Juniper with four hot pink suitcases stuffed to the brim full of clothes, and Serena, who was changed out of her fancy date night look and now wearing an old pair of Juniper's jeans, sneakers, and a pale blue shirt with a muffin graphic on it.

"All right," beamed a satisfied Juniper, "We're ready."

"Is that a muffin on your shirt?" asked Oliver.

"You're not the only one who can wear food inspired clothes, butt-bag," Juniper replied.

"Yeah, Oliver," said Serena, "Don't you like my muffin top?" she said through laughter. It really wasn't that funny of a joke. Puns were *my* thing. Stay in your lane, muffin man.

"Girls are confusing."

"Are you sure it's that, or is it because boys are dumb?" retorted Juniper.

"Stop waltzing, buddy," I told him. I grabbed the Lycan Stone and stuffed him into my backpack and slung it over my right shoulder. Then the four of us walked downstairs, out the front door evading swings from Georgia, and finally, outside to the driveway.

"You mind if I drive?" I asked Serena.

"No, go ahead. It's just my car that I bought myself with all my life's savings, hopes and dreams," she teased.

"So, that's a yes then?"

"Yeah, sure. Somehow, I feel like you would be an annoying backseat driver."

I got in the driver's seat, this time with Serena in the passenger's seat beside me. Oliver and Juniper sat in the back with her volcano of suitcases sitting in the middle of the seat as a divider between the two.

After a few quick minutes of driving, I pulled into the driveway of a small townhouse on a quiet street.

We stepped out of Serena's red car and onto the concrete driveway.

"Zade," said Oliver, "what are we doing here?"

"Where exactly is '*here?*'" wondered Serena.

"'*Here'* would be my house," I said.

15
ZADE
Family reunion

I was both excited and nervous to see my parents again. After all, it had been a while since I yelled at them and snuck out, only to return and discover that Mom was sick.

I led the way to the door, followed by Oliver, Juniper, and Serena, and knocked.

The brown door opened and revealed a familiar man standing behind it, slightly backlit from the dimly lit living room.

Dad stood and stared at me for what felt like five minutes before embracing me in a rib-crushing bear hug of pure love and relief– relief that quickly turned into rage.

"Zade Anthony Corey, you are in *so* much trouble. Don't you ever pull anything like that again," he scolded me. "And for the record, I nailed your window shut. I haven't decided how long to ground you for."

"Sorry Dad, but at least I'm home now, right?" I said. "And as much as I'd love to be grounded, I can't. Something big is happening."

"I think I'll get you a shock collar for Christmas this year."

"I think I'd prefer coal," I protested, walking past my dad and into the entry of our home. Oliver, Juniper and Serena followed my lead.

The house hadn't changed at all since I last left it. Same oak panels, same shag carpeting, same staircase to the right, kitchen to the left, living room straight ahead.

Dad closed the door and turned to face the four of us. "I don't know if you've heard about your mom or not, but she's not been well ever since you left."

"Where is she?" I asked.

Dad led us deeper into the house and into the living room, where a tired Nina was laying on her side on a brown leather couch. I rushed to her side and knelt down to her level.

Mom's usually neatly combed blond hair looked as if it hadn't been brushed in weeks. That, or maybe it was just static electricity from the couch.

"You're home," she smiled up at me. Her voice was soft and weak, and sounded forced.

"Yeah. I am," I smiled.

She reached out and held my face in her hands, running her thumbs along my new scars. "My sweet child, what has this world done to *you*? Please don't go ever again."

"Not even to college?" I questioned her, raising an eyebrow. "I remember you telling me that I have to go to college."

"I'll home-college you," she proposed.

I wrapped my arms around my mom and embraced her in a gentle hug that was long overdue.

"I'm sorry I left on a bad note. I just needed to get out in the world. Mom, something's happening. Something really bad is happening, and Kyra is at the center of it," I told her, pulling away to look at my mom. "I'm gonna have to leave again, and I don't know when I'll be back."

Her expression saddened. “But you just got back…”

“I know, but if I don’t go, there’s gonna be a lot of chaos,"I explained.

“Please.....”

“Nina,” said Lyall, “Zade has a job to do. We have to let him do it.”

“Yeah. We’re going to Massachusetts,” said Serena.

“I’m sorry,” said Mom, “but I don’t recall who you are.”

“Serena Putnam. I’m a friend.”

I was afraid a fight would break out at any moment. I could tell my parents sensed that Serena was in no way at all a Shifter, but I decided to put my worries to the side so no unnecessary attention would be brought to light about the subject.

“All right,” I said, abruptly standing up, “let’s get this freak show on the go.”

16
SERENA
Hopefully Little Red survives the wolves

I sat in the back of my car next to Oliver. Zade was at the wheel again, and Juniper sat shotgun diagonal from me. Her many suitcases had been moved to the trunk to make the car less cramped.

It had been one full day of driving, and we had managed to make it all the way to Omaha, Nebraska. Zade, Oliver and Juniper had all agreed not to stop at a gas station anywhere in this town for a reason they had not yet explained to me.

Zade agreed, after a long argument, to spend the night in a local hotel, beings we had another full day of driving ahead of us. After tonight, we would only have one more day to get to Massachusetts and stop this guy called Derek.

We pulled into a parking lot for a Country Inn and Suites. Zade parked somewhere between a pickup truck and a sports car, and shut off the engine. He stuffed the vehicle's keys into a pocket in his beloved backpack.

As we stepped out of my car, I couldn't help but feel that my bad feeling was only getting stronger. Something bad was either happening or was about to, and when I glanced over in Zade's direction, I could tell that he felt it, too, though he hid it well. Why did nobody else seem to notice it?

Zade opened the trunk and grabbed the four bright pink bags of Juniper's, each loaded and weighed down with tons of clothing and other supplies the girl brought with her. Each bag had to weigh at least seven pounds each. He handed the smallest bag to Juniper, and proceeded to carry the rest with him into the hotel.

I didn't know how he didn't struggle with those heavy bags. Looking at Zade, he didn't have a very muscular build. He was built tall and lean, but not scrawny. Just your typical gangly seventeen-year-old boy. But if there's one thing I had learned from these three strange people was that appearances were deceiving, and what you see is not what you get.

I stood by the side of my small red car and watched the trio cross the parking lot.

"Well, Little Red?" Zade said, stopping and turning in my direction. "Are you coming or what? We don't have all day."

Little Red. I liked that.

"Yeah!" I ran up to the three Shifters. "Do you need some help with those bags?"

17
ZADE
I'm an alien

I was getting increasingly agitated as every second passed by.

Me and my friends were caught up in a line to the front desk, and all I wanted to do was get checked in as soon as possible and get this day over with. Our deadline required us to be in Massachusetts by tomorrow, and at this rate, we were going to miss it.

The other issue was that if, and once, we did make it to Salem, where exactly were we supposed to go?

I was hoping that once I crawled into one of those weird smelling, really uncomfortable hotel beds I'd have another one of my death dreams and everything would be sorted out and we'd celebrate with ice cream and sprinkles.

After a long wait, the family of four in front of us left, and we were up next.

I set down two of Juniper's bags. Serena had helped me carry in the other one. "We'd like a room, please," I said.

"Uh-uh," Juniper disagreed, "I am *not* sharing a room with him." She pointed her thumb back at Oliver.

"Fine," I sighed, "Make that two rooms."

"I'm going to need to see some ID," said the front desk lady.

I dropped my backpack onto the counter and rummaged through it until I found my driver's license. "This is all I've got with me," I said.

"That'll do. And how long do you intend to stay?"

"Just for tonight. We'll be out of here by at least noon," I answered her.

"That's about one hundred three, then."

"One hundred three!" I cried. "There goes our money."

The lady, whose nametag read Alice, began punching in information on her computer.

"Zade," she said, "that's a cool name. It's just like...... wait a second." Alice grabbed my right wrist that was resting on the countertop and pulled my sweater sleeve back, revealing the black crescent moon shaped mark. "You *are* him," she whispered.

"Uhhh..." I stumbled, "No I'm not? Who exactly are you?"

"Don't worry!" assured Alice, "I'm not against you! I'm a Shifter myself, and I think the Council is wrong to go after you."

"Wait, they're after me now?"

"They've contacted Shifters everywhere to be on the lookout for you, though there are a few, like me, who don't always believe their stories. Of course people are going to recognize you! You're like some legendary outlaw. Marshall, Michigan is all that's on the news now. The anchors keep telling the story about the blue fire, thinking it has something to do with aliens. What idiots! But the explosion did do a number on the town, though. Some nearby buildings were partly destroyed, and there were a couple of car accidents on the highway, causing multiple jams, but no one was seriously injured. How have you not heard any of this? What are you guys even doing in the Wildes' Territory anyways?"

All of Alice's talking was starting to give me a headache. I already didn't feel good. I was a tad dizzy, but I figured it was from being overtired. "Look, can we just get a room, please? We have places to be," I said.

"Oh! Yeah, yeah! I'm sorry, I just got a little excited. You're on the third story, rooms thirty-three and thirty-four." Alice slid me the two keycards.

"Thank you," I nodded.

"And about the price," said Alice. "You don't need to worry about it. It's on the house," she smiled.

I smiled back at her, put on my trusty backpack, and picked up Juniper's luggage. As we started for the elevator, I couldn't help but feel like something was wrong. Juniper's bags somehow felt heavier than before, and it was becoming increasingly difficult to carry them. Walking was even starting to feel like a chore, and with every step I took, the weaker I felt.

Juniper pressed the up button on the elevator and the metallic doors opened almost immediately, beings there were no other people in it.

My nose was beginning to irritate me. It felt weird, and it was not making my head feel any better. You better cut the crap, nose.

Oliver, Juniper and Serena all shuffled inside, followed by me. We set down our luggage on the floor.

I leaned against the elevator's walls, resisting the urge to just fall to the floor and be done with the day.

"Are you okay there, bud?" asked Oliver. "You don't quite seem yourself."

"I'll be fine." I wiped my aching nose, and when I looked down at my hand, it had blood on it. I had a nosebleed.

"Great," I sighed and wiped my hand on my jeans.

"It doesn't look like you're fine to me," argued Juniper.

"What's wrong with you?" wondered Oliver.

"Where do I begin to answer that question. I think a shorter list would be what's right with me," I joked.

"You know that's not what I meant," said Oliver.

The elevator doors slid open, showing a hallway full of numbered, uniform doors lined up from left to right on the cream-colored walls.

I took one step forward and it all came crashing down...... literally. Everything seemed to happen in slow motion. My vision blurred as I fell. I watched the floor getting closer and closer to my face. I was sure I would hit it at any moment now, but before I could collide with the ground, I felt an arm hook under my left armpit and pull me upwards to my knees at an awkward angle that was in no way at all comfortable.

I could faintly hear my friends' voices in the background calling out my name. I felt myself being pulled up, and my left arm was slung around Oliver's neck, giving me better support.

I was carried out of the elevator and into the hallway. I felt my backpack be removed from my shoulders. From what I was able to see, Juniper and Serena had taken all the luggage, including my backpack, and were desperately trying to juggle carrying heavy bags and what to do with me.

After what seemed like ten minutes of stumbling and Oliver almost dropping me over and over, Juniper finally found our room and swiped the keycard through the slot. The door made a clicking sound and Juniper opened it. Oliver drug me in, followed by Serena and Juniper.

He helped me sit on the first of the queen-sized beds, and I immediately fell over on my back with arms sprawled out. I didn't have the willpower to sit back up.

My eyelids felt heavy, and I struggled to keep them open. My vision was slowly going black. I didn't want to pass out, but it was becoming increasingly difficult to stay conscious.

Juniper rushed to my side with a plastic bottle of water in hand. She sat me up and forced the jug into my shaky hands. "Drink," she commanded.

I obeyed. The cold water refreshed me, and my senses slowly but surely started to come back. I was able to see and hear properly again.

"What is wrong with you?" exclaimed Juniper.

"I don't know what happened. Maybe I'm just overtired from driving too much."

"Well, whatever it is, just stay here and we'll get settled in," told Juniper.

She and Serena gathered up all the pink suitcases and left the room.

I propped myself up against the headboard of the bed and tucked myself under the covers.

Overall, the room wasn't very large. I was on the bed closest to the door and wall of the bathroom whereas the second bed was next to sliding window doors, which led to a balcony outside. There was a pretty decent sized TV across from the set of beds, and to the right of that was one of those doors that lead to the other room, which was most likely the girls' room. There wasn't much else in the room besides a single nightstand between the two queen-sized beds with a lamp on it, an old chair in the corner on the left side of the TV, and a couple decorative pieces on the walls.

"Dude," said Oliver, "don't ever do that again. I am not tall *or* strong enough to support you. I think I put my back out..."

"Okay, grandma, next time I'll try harder not to pass out when I'm passing out," I joked with him.

Oliver gave me two thumbs up, then went right on back to massaging his lower back.

There was a knock on the connecting door.

"Don't expect me to get it," I said.

"Fine." Oliver strode over to the door connecting their hotel room to the girls' and opened it. Juniper stood in the doorway with a colorful striped swimsuit and a blue cover-up on.

"So," she started, "Serena didn't want to go swimming in the indoor pool tonight, so I guess I have to ask you."

"You're inviting *me* to hang out with *you?*" said a surprised Oliver. "You never want to hang out with me."

"I still don't want to, but I don't think it would be a bright idea to bring Zade along after what just happened a few minutes ago. I just don't want to go by myself," stated Juniper.

"We literally just got settled in, and you want to go swimming now?"

"It helps to clear my head. I need to do some thinking," she explained.

"All right," agreed Oliver. "Just give me two minutes to change."

She leaned against the doorframe and crossed her arms over her chest. "The clock is ticking."

Oliver rushed to my backpack and flung out random things that included, but weren't limited to: three shirts, the Lycan Stone who screamed as he was flung across the room, and a couple granola bars. He finally found his pair of swim trunks that he had snuck into my backpack a long time ago, just in case we stopped at a hotel such as this one. Then, he ran as fast as his legs could carry him across the room and into the bathroom.

"I'm really not looking forward to seeing him shirtless," Juniper complained.

"Yeah, well, you might want to wear a pair of shades. He's pretty pale," I suggested. "His heritage kind of makes it inevitable."

"I really wish you could come, too," said Juniper. "Are you feeling any better?"

"Yeah. Whatever it was that happened is gone now," I lied. My head was killing me. My vision was blurred, and my stomach churned from the immense and excruciating pain.

I could tell that Juniper could see straight through me, but she just gave me a nervous look and smiled. "Yeah. Okay."

Oliver violently thrusted open the bathroom door and burst out, wearing his green swim trunks with little sharks on them. "I feel FABULOUS!" he screeched.

"This was a mistake," Juniper sighed to herself.

I winced. Oliver's high-pitched screech felt like a blade just sliced through my ears, straight through my brain. Contrary to popular belief, I do have one.

I began to tap my fingers against my legs in a rhythm, counting every individual tap— a strategy I had developed to help me cope with loud sounds or other intense stimuli that hurt my sensitive Shifter senses.

"OLIVER!" I yelled, getting more and more agitated with every failed attempt to count over the noises. "Shut up, or so help me I will throttle you and watch the light slowly fade out of your eyes," I snarled.

"Geez, dude, that's a little dark," Oliver whimpered.

"It will be!" I warned him.

"Zade..." said Juniper.

"GET OUT!" I roared, igniting both my palms with my newfound blue fire.

Oliver and Juniper scrambled to the door and quickly slammed it behind them.

My magic blue fire set off the smoke detector, which then in turn set off the sprinklers, drenching me, not to mention the loud chirping noises the smoke detector was emitting.

I covered my ears and screamed so loud that I was sure June and Oliver could hear me from all the way down the hall.

I closed my palms, extinguishing my flames. "You've got to be kidding me!"

Lycan laughed maniacally from under the pile of shirts Oliver had tossed on the old chair. Granola bars laid around him like a shrine to a hangry god.

"I *will* smash you," I threatened him.

Serena ran into our room through the open connecting door and stopped right in the doorway. With hands on her hips, she watched as the water spewed out of the sprinklers as the annoying chirp from the smoke detector rang throughout the entire room. "You've got some explaining to do," was all she said.

18
DEREK
Kyra screwed it up

I heard a knock on my hotel door. I hoped it wasn't the pizza man who got the wrong room number again, or I would scar that man emotionally and make him cry for his mommy.

I got up from my spot on the edge of the hotel bed and paused the news. All that was on it was my humiliation anyways. This time I would not fail. This time I had the moon.

When I opened the door, Kyra strode inside and quickly shut the door. Guess the plane got in a little earlier.

"Took you long enough."

"Well, hello to you, too." Kyra walked deeper into the room and sat down on the office chair in one corner of the room. "I'm fine, other than being choked," she snarked.

"Sorry." I pushed a strand of her black hair behind her ear. "What I meant to say was that I missed you." I gently kissed Kyra's lips.

"That's more like it," she smiled.

"Did you bring the coin?" I asked her.

"Well, it would be kinda pointless for me to travel all the way here without it." Kyra pulled a small golden coin out of her back pocket and tossed it towards me.

I snatched it out of the air and studied the designs on each of the two sides. "Finally," I muttered to myself.

"I'll get it back, right?" she asked. "I promised my dad I wouldn't lose it."

"It *is* the Coin of the Alpha's, and, last I checked, you're the alpha."

I pocketed the coin, and Kyra wrapped her arms around my neck and swayed with me. "Oh, I wish you could've seen me that night. It was the biggest moment of my life– I wish you could've celebrated with me. Mom had a chocolate fountain," she recalled, smiling at the memory.

"I'm a lone wolf, darling," I smiled at her. "Okay, but seriously, I didn't want to start anything with your pack on your big night."

"You're an honorary member by now," she said.

"Maybe so," I said, still hanging onto Kyra, "But I don't belong there. I'm going to fix the way things are, Kyra."

Kyra stopped swaying now. "What do you mean?"

"Remember how the Council trapped Lycan?"

"Yeah, I know the story," said Kyra. "I also know that they forced a Shifter to acquire the black magic, and after Lycan was banished and they got what they wanted, killed him because it created an unbalance. That's, like, the whole thing the Ancients were about preventing before they disappeared. It's not a good idea."

"It's a perfect idea," I argued. "Even the moon makes mistakes. Trust me, Kyra– we're fulfilling a destiny, here! This is something I have to do."

Kyra looked into my eyes, her almond-shaped brown ones searching for something in my face. "Okay," she said. "Okay."

"Now, did you bring me his blood?"

"Seriously, Derek. This whole thing with Zade and magic has turned into an obsession. *I'm* the Corey sibling you're supposed to care about!" complained Kyra.

I leaned in and kissed her, holding the sides of her face in my hands. "There."

"That's more like it," she smiled.

"Now," I began again, "You were going to answer my question?"

"Um," Kyra cleared her throat. "No..."

"You've got to be kidding me. You're kidding me, right?"

"No."

"That's an important part of the recipe, Kyra, and you screwed it up. How does it feel knowing that you screwed up something so badly, you screwed it down?" I yelled.

"Look, Derek, I know I messed up, but I killed a member of the Council," told Kyra. She pulled a small container out from her back pocket with a red liquid in it. "I got *his* blood."

"No!" I argued. "That won't work, that won't work at all! It *has* to be Zade's!"

"The power is *that* limited?" Kyra questioned. "You have to have the Zenith's blood?"

"Yes, or I wouldn't be angry!"

I began to pace around the hotel room, not knowing what to do. I had everything except the main ingredient that would make it all work. If I couldn't get Zade's blood, I would have to wait years to pull this stunt again, and I was having none of that. I just had to figure out a way to make sure Zade showed up where I needed him to be. That's when the solution hit me.

"That's it!" I exclaimed. "This is kind of a longshot, but, if I can pull it off, should work out to be just fine."

"So, what's this big idea?" asked Kyra.

"I've already got almost everything for tomorrow, and I'm so close to the location I need to be in that I'm sure I've already created a small part of that unbalance. Zade should be feeling it by now, making him an even more dangerous and explosive ticking time bomb. He'll know where to be. He'll find me."

19
SERENA
I'm an honorary wolf

I glared at Zade, staring directly into his big blue puppy dog eyes. He stared right back into mine, almost like he was challenging me. It was the strangest thing. Then I remembered: he was a wolf, and there was no way he would be the first to look away. Come to think of it, Oliver never made direct eye contact with Zade for more than three seconds, and only Juniper was brave enough to do so. I turned away, hoping to ease some of the tension in the room. Just as I had thought, the second my eyes unlocked with his, he seemed less guarded. These were strange people.

It was a good thing I had paid attention to that one life science lesson about animals and their social habits back when I lived in Alaska. As a kid, I moved a lot, and I absolutely hated it. My parents were both businesspeople, and their company required them to jump around a lot. Besides being born and living the majority of my life in Nome, Alaska, our most recent move was from our home of three years in Juno, Alaska, to Salem, Oregon. My parents had recently quit their jobs so that they wouldn't have to relocate again. That's where they were now; a business trip with their new boss for a whole new job opportunity that wouldn't require anymore moving.

I looked around the hotel room. The sprinklers had finally stopped, but the smoke detector would still let out an occasional chirp every once in a while.

"What's the story?" I asked him.

"I guess you could say that I'm a bit of a hothead," shrugged Zade. Terrible pun, really.

"That's still no reason to set the hotel ablaze."

"I know. I don't know what came over me. I just got so angry..."

I made my way to Oliver's bed and sat down sideways near the headboard, directly across from Zade.

"I'm still learning how to control this Zenith stuff, and I've never been a quick learner. What are we going to tell the staff when they ask why our room smells like a wet dog that was set on fire? '*Oops, I'm sorry, the microwave malfunctioned,*'" Zade teased.

"I think that would be our best option," I agreed, still being careful not to meet eyes with Zade. I did not want to be on this guy's crap-list.

"Maybe. So how are things going with Oliver?"

"Good. The guy's great. Really nervous, though."

"I think you can fix that. The poor guy doesn't have a clue of what to say to you. He adores you," said Zade.

"Oh, well, that's good to hear. It'd be kind of awkward if he hated me."

"This may sound cheesy, but I just want you to know that he can be broken easily, and if you hurt him, I *will* hurt you," Zade stared into my eyes, making his dominance clear.

I swallowed. "Noted."

Just then, Juniper burst into the hotel room laughing, followed by Oliver, who looked like he'd just seen a ghost.

"Oh, oh, oooooooooooooooooohhhhhhh!" Juniper doubled over laughing.

"It's NOT funny!" protested Oliver.

"What's the problem here?" Zade rose slowly off the mattress, still just a little unsteady.

Oliver looked like he was about to burst into tears at any moment. They hadn't been gone very long. What happened?

He pointed at Juniper. "This… this MONSTER tried to drown me!"

"I was just standing in the pool and he just so happened to be underneath my arms," told Juniper.

"Yeah, and while you were busy doing that, some little six-year-old boy got so scared and peed in the pool!"

"Juniper. You don't attempt to kill friends in public. If you have a score to settle, you do it later," said Zade. "And Oliver, don't be such an easy target. Stand your ground and don't let Juniper push you around so much. I couldn't go on without either one of you."

I was amazed at how wolf-like these people were. I hadn't taken into account how they interacted before, but it was very obvious to me now. They had their own social statuses amongst themselves, and genuinely cared for one another to the point of aggression. Or maybe that's their way of having fun, which was kind of a scary thought.

"It's getting pretty late and we have another full day of driving ahead of us tomorrow," said Zade. "I think we should get ready for bed. It's been a long day."

He grabbed his red plaid pajama bottoms and a gray t-shirt and made his way to the bathroom to change.

I left to the other room to do the same. I was exhausted. All day cooped up in a car with angry beat-up teenagers was not the way I'd imagined this road trip would be. There were minimal stops made in the time between Salem to Omaha.

I decided to sleep in the muffin top shirt, but I put on a pair of pink capri sweatpants borrowed from Juniper.

My usually straight red hair was still a little curly from last night, and it reeked of hairspray, but I was too tired to do anything but sleep at the moment. I crawled into the bed that was the closest to the balcony. Shortly after, Oliver walked in, sporting a gray pair of sweatpants matched with a huge fluffy white robe that engulfed and covered the rest of him. I couldn't see anything below the middle of his neck and above his knees.

"What are you doing in here?" I asked him.

"Well," he responded, "Zade and June are in the other room, so I figured I could spend some quality time with you before we went to bed. Besides, I wanted to show you something cool." He led me out onto the balcony.

It was nice to get some fresh air, and looking down below at all the cars rushing by was strangely relaxing, but Oliver by my side made me feel even more comfortable. He was the only remotely familiar thing here.

"Look at how beautiful the moon is," he said, pointing at the almost full moon.

"Yeah," I agreed. "It's so peaceful."

"Now howl."

"What?" I exclaimed. "They'll think we're crazy!"

"Who cares? It's the best stress reliever you'll ever try. Just howl with me!" Oliver threw back his head and emitted the longest and loudest howl I'd ever heard.

Oliver nodded his head at me, and I tossed my head back and let out my very best attempt at a wolf howl, and together we cried to the moon.

20
ZADE
Follow your dreams, especially if your sister keeps dying

I cried out in pain as the black fire scorched and burned my tan skin, but no matter how loud I would scream, no one seemed to hear me. I fell to my knees, screaming in pain as the flames engulfed me. I wasn't strong enough to fight it off.

Suddenly, everything shifted, and the fire was gone. I now stood at the bottom of a hill. I climbed up it to see the black silhouette of a man toss a coin into the air. I watched as the coin fell back down in slow-motion, flipping through the air, only to be intercepted by the man.

The second the coin touched the figure's flesh, I felt an immediate stabbing pain in my upper back, crumpling me to my knees. Then the scene changed again, and when I looked up, I saw my sister in place of the silhouette. I tried to get up, but the pain between my shoulder blades made it difficult and agonizing.

"You're a monster. A freak! Get away from me!" Kyra screamed as she backed away, desperately covering a wound in her chest.

"Kyra..." I inched forward, but found I couldn't get any closer. I turned to look at my right foot, which was clamped in shackles and bound to... I don't even know what. The chains were attached to something buried deep in the ground. Well, not necessarily *something.* It was probably *someone.*

I heard footsteps getting closer and closer. I had no idea whose they were, but something in me knew I didn't want to stick around to find out.

"Help me!" I pleaded with Kyra, pulling at the chains on my ankle.

Kyra ignored me, backing farther and farther away, still clutching her bleeding chest. "Leave me alone!"

"Help me!" My voice was frantic and shaky. "Kyra! Help me!"

The footsteps got louder and louder, and the sound seemed to echo through my head.

"You did this to me!" Kyra accused. "You're a monster!" She slumped to the ground.

I had *thought* she was talking to me, but she slumped to the ground, looking ever so slightly behind me. I jerked and tugged at my restraints to no avail. The footsteps stopped, and I felt a cold hand clamp around my neck. Long claws pressed tightly against my throat. I froze. There was no escape.

Whatever was now behind me whispered one phrase in a cold, harsh voice that sent chills down my spine and made every hair on the back of my neck stand on end.

"Time's up."

21
ZADE
I'm a really bad friend

I clawed at my ankle and screamed until my throat felt raw and bloody, but even then I didn't stop.

The sound wasn't entirely me. A choir of voices and shrill shrieks came out with my voice, and my skin erupted into goosebumps and chills.

Oliver sat up in bed, screaming as well.

Juniper and Serena rushed into the room. "What's wrong?" asked Juniper. "Zade, what's wrong?" she demanded. I wish I didn't know the answer.

Kyra was going to die.

"Oliver, shut up!" yelled Serena. "Why are you guys screaming?"

"I heard Zade scream and I got scared," he explained.

"That," said Juniper, panting, "Was *not* just a scream. That was hell being unleashed via your mouth. Zade, what we heard was *not* normal. It was like hundreds of screams overlaid on top of your own. It was like when Twitch died."

When my breathing returned to normal, I began to speak. "Bad... bad dream." My voice sounded shaky and weak, even to me. I hated that dream. I hated that dream *so much.*

Juniper placed a hand on my forehead. "Zade, you're burning up," she said.

"Fire will do that to ya," I said.

"Fire!" asked an alarmed Juniper, "What fire?"

"Bad dream," I said again.

"Gee, I don't think it's possible to be any more specific."

"I don't wanna talk about it," I said. I hadn't had that nightmare since before we went to Michigan. I thought it was over, and here it was again, back and worse than ever. It always, *always* ended in her death. Always. That scream meant something. I shook myself back to reality and continued, "However, we've got a general direction to travel tomorrow. Gallows Hill."

"Oh no," refused Oliver. "No, no, no, no, no. Seriously? You're serious? Dude, that is *not* a peaceful place to be."

"Don't you think I know?" I yelled, still unsettled from the dream. "It's not my first choice, but at this point we don't really have one."

"I just thought–"

"NO! No one cares what you thought, Oliver!"

"Dude, what gives?" Oliver shouted back.

"You think I can just pick where we go? That I can just turn my head off and be done with this? Hate to break it to you, moron, but that's not how things work."

"You're an insult to Zeniths."

"Oliver!" screamed an angry Juniper.

"What? It's not my fault his own family didn't even think he could be it!"

"Oh, *I'M* the one with family issues?" I roared. "That's rich. When was the last time you actually *talked* to your parents?"

I knew that was a touchy subject for Oliver, but if he was going to bring up my home life, I was going to, too. I am more than capable of fighting fire with fire.

I knew my parents cared for Kyra and I, and still do, but I never fit in their mold. I was the Zenith and desperately wanted to be it, too. But if I so much as even looked at fire, I was scolded. They never wanted me to learn, they only wanted me to blend in. It's the Council's fault, really. If they weren't so eager to kill me, I could know everything about my abilities and how to use them by now, and I wouldn't be in this mess. Maybe I could force the nightmares to stop if I knew why they started in the first place.

"One more insult out of your mouth and I swear," threatened Oliver.

"Or you swear *what?*" I mocked him. "You'll give me a papercut? Oh, no! Look out! Here comes big bad Oliver, and he's got a piece of paper with him! I'm so scared!"

Oliver glared at me. "Yeah, but who's the real winner, scar-face," Oliver shot back. "Your beloved sissy-poo gave you those boo-boos on your face, and your mommy didn't kiss it all better. All you've ever been and all you'll ever be is trouble."

"My mom is *sick,*" I snarled.

Oliver rolled his eyes. "Yeah, that's why you stayed. Oh, wait..."

I balled my hands into flaming blue fists and glared at Oliver, approaching him slowly.

"Okay, Zade, that's enough," Oliver said nervously, trying to keep his composure. But the look in his eyes and the crack in his voice told me he was fearful. That was good. But I couldn't just let Oliver get away with insulting me without a warning.

I grinned and extinguished the fire in my palms, but that wasn't the end of it. I twitched my hands by my side, phasing my nails into long, sharp wolf claws. "Let me ask you a question," I said. "Are you *afraid* of me, Oliver?"

"Zade," began Oliver, "I get it. You can stop now, I'm sorry. You're scaring me, dude."

"You *should* be scared of *me*!" With all my might, I clawed Oliver in the face, cutting him along his left jawline and chin.

The amount of force in the attack was enough to knock Oliver over, and he fell back into the curtains, hitting his back on the heater and holding his hands against his bleeding cut.

He looked up at me, and the look of utter betrayal in his dark green eyes shook me to my core.

Reality hit me like a truck. I looked down at my shaking palms and slowly backed up.

I felt like I was in another one of my awful nightmares, but the only difference was that I couldn't wake up from this one, and I'd have to live with what I'd just done. There was no interpreting it. It was what it was.

What the hell is happening to me?!

Oliver dizzily stood up, utterly horrified at what had just happened.

"Oliver, I—" I stuttered, looking up from my bloodstained claws and back at Oliver.

"Save it, Zade," Oliver snarled. He stormed past me, purposely plowing into my shoulder as he exited the room. "I thought we were friends."

22
JUNIPER
Eyes are the window to the soul…
Oh no

Oliver stormed out of the hotel room and into ours, followed by Serena, who was desperately trying to comfort him.

Zade rested his elbows on his knees and pulled at his black locks of hair. "Juniper," he muttered, "Juniper, I don't know what came over me. I don't know what to do. I've never fought with Oliver before. What's wrong with me? This isn't normal."

"It's okay. There's a lot going on right now," I reassured him. I sat down cross-legged on the bed across from him and held his hands in mine. I always loved to hold his hands. They were always warm. "Everything is going to work out." I lifted my gaze to meet with Zade's and gasped.

"What's wrong?" wondered Zade.

What I saw in Zade's eyes worried me. Eric was right; his eyes were scary. They didn't look like his normal deep blue puppy eyes. They were similar, but unsettling all the same. They were his usual dark blue color except the outer ring, which was a very dark and pronounced black. The black color seemed to seep into his ocean-blue eyes, like little lines of darkness extending from the edge, reaching midway to his pupil.

"Nothing. Nothing's wrong." I scooted closer to Zade and kissed him.

He pulled away. "Juniper, what's wrong?" he repeated.

I gave in and told him. "Your eyes," I whispered. I guess I thought if I said it quiet enough it wouldn't be as big of a deal.

"What about my eyes?" Zade asked nervously. He climbed off the bed and made his way to the bathroom, trailed by me.

He looked in the mirror and inhaled sharply. "How long have they been like this?"

Zade's reaction was strange; almost as if he'd been expecting something weird to happen.

"I don't know," I replied honestly. "I just noticed them now. Whatever's happening is directly affecting you, and not in a good way. That scream was really something, Zade."

Zade stared even longer at his reflection. "Juniper..." he started, his voice shaky, "What... what's this black eye-shaped mark and why didn't you tell me about it?" he asked, pointing a finger at the middle of his forehead.

I spun him around and examined his face. "Zade, there's nothing there. There wasn't before, and there isn't now," I said.

"You can't see it?"

I shook my head no. "There's nothing there. There was never anything there."

Zade turned back to the mirror and blinked. "There's nothing there..." he whispered to himself. "It's gone..."

"I think you're just overtired," I said. "You're just tired and your eyes are playing tricks on you, that's all."

"Yeah, maybe. You're probably right. Can we just kiss again?"

I smiled. "Get your butt over here, hothead."

Zade pulled me close to him and we kissed. I wrapped my arms around his neck while he held my head in his hands. "Juniper," he whispered, grinning his sideways grin, "I love you."

"I love you, too, you big dork," I beamed, "Even if you are a little scary."

"I don't think anybody could beat you."

"Just shut up and kiss me, doofus."

We pulled away, still holding onto each other.

"Well, I suppose we better get going," said Zade.

"Zade, it's literally five in the morning. You told the lady we'd be out by noon," I argued.

"Exactly. We'll be out before noon. Emphasis on *before*."

Just because he has nightmares that means the rest of us can't sleep? Dang. "That's quite a difference in time."

"It's for getting ready," Zade explained.

I sighed. "Whatever you say."

"Besides, we have another full day of driving ahead of us. If we want to get to Gallows Hill by tonight, we have to leave ASAP."

Ever since the fight with Derek and Kyra almost a month ago, Zade seemed different. He wasn't his usual happy-go-lucky, pun-loving self. He was more temperamental and dejected. Something was going on, and it was enough to shake the Zenith.

"I'll go get ready then," I sighed.

I left Zade's side and strolled into Serena and I's hotel room. I walked past Oliver and made sure to give him the death stare. I know Zade wasn't very nice, but it wasn't really *Zade.*

When I entered the bathroom, I cussed. Suddenly the only thing that mattered was me. I forgot my hair curler. I knew I was missing something important!

Dang. Now my hair was going to suck. My day was ruined before it even started.

I continued to angrily pull myself together. I pulled on a clean pair of skinny jeans, a white tank top, and a brown cropped leather jacket with matching leather boots– my favorite pair, of course. I fastened Lycan's golden necklace around my neck. It was, after all, a one-of-a-kind accessory.

I spent another hour trying to tame my blond locks without my curler until I got them to lay just the way I wanted, but they weren't as curled as I would've liked. Just my normal, wavy mane. How disappointing.

"I'm ready," I said, stepping out of the bathroom, lugging one of my pink suitcases along with me into a room full of impatient friends who were not as fabulous as me.

Serena wore a purple long sleeve shirt with a wolf face imprinted in black ink on the front, paired with jeans and black ankle-high boots— all things borrowed from me.

Zade was wearing a pair of jeans, his usual sneakers, and a gray three-quarter length sleeve t-shirt, which complemented his tan skin that was a nice result of his mixed Inuit and Norwegian genetics. He looked hot, (pun intended).

Lastly, Oliver was dressed in a red Nike 'Just Do It' t-shirt and a pair of denim jeans as well. Wow, a real step up from sweatpants. He wasn't wearing his usual green beanie, so his straight brown hair was free to be all up in his face.

I pulled a knife sheathed in leather out of a pocket from my suitcase. "Catch." I threw the knife at Serena, who, despite being absolutely terrified of the weapon flying towards her, caught it. What? It was sheathed. "I've got my favorite pair of boots on today and I'm ready to stomp the life out of our enemies!" I grinned.

23
OLIVER
We're all about to get our butts kicked

I was not amused. It was way too early for anything to be happening. Plus, the exchanging of words between Zade and I this morning, and the new, dull ache in my jaw didn't do anything to lighten my mood.

I stared out the window from behind the driver's seat. I debated whether or not to kick it, beings Zade was driving, but decided against it. I had no intentions of dying today. Not from a car crash, not from a furious Juniper, and definitely not from a combustible frenemy.

Speaking of Juniper, before we took off from the hotel, she had pulled me aside and told me something about Zade that sent a shiver down my spine. Zade had complained about 'seeing' a black mark in the shape of an eye in the middle of his forehead, and Juniper couldn't see a thing, but he was insistent that it was there.

Now, normally I would just let the incident slide and brush it off as another weird Zade moment, except this time it was something serious that I knew the meaning behind:

The black third eye was the mark of a Shadow. The one they call Fenrir. You don't mess with Fenrir. You don't even *think* about Fenrir.

I shook the thought out of my head and turned to face Serena, who was seated behind the passenger's seat, behind where Juniper was sitting. Zade's backpack served as the divider in the middle seat. I wanted to sit closer to her, but I didn't want to rush the relationship. At the moment, we were nothing special. After all, we had only been on, like, one real date and had just barely gotten to know each other, unlike Zade and Juniper, who had known each other since kindergarten, and it was obvious to anyone that those two would've eventually paired up. They had a history together. Serena, well, I had history *class* with her. I'd only known of her as of last month.

I liked having her with, though, and not just because we had to have her along because I told her about all Shifters and now we had to keep a watchful eye on her to make sure she didn't blab about anything. She was good company. When Zade and Juniper were having their *moments*, I had someone to gag at the scene with me.

"We're almost there," said Zade.

It was dark now, but the car ride didn't seem to last as long as yesterday. I didn't feel so... cramped. We left the hotel around six in the morning, and we were already in Massachusetts. We had only five minutes to pull this thing off before the moon reached its peak in the night sky at midnight.

Zade pulled into a parking spot and shut off the car. He rubbed his head and groaned. "This is definitely where we're supposed to be," he said. His voice sounded forced, like he was in a lot of pain, and it physically hurt to do anything. I really didn't feel all that bad for him this time.

"Serena," I started, "when we get out of whatever's about to happen, will you go on a second date with me?"

"I'm counting on it," she smiled.

Whoa, that never happens.

"All right, guys," said Zade, "Keep in mind that it's Halloween night, and there will be a lot of people here. Innocent people who have nothing to do with us and our problems. No matter what, no bystander gets hurt, understand?"

I nodded along with Juniper and Serena.

"Okay then."

I noticed a pair of red eyes glowing through Zade's backpack. I unzipped the bag, pulled out the Lycan stone and set it down on the middle seat.

"*About time!*" *hollered Lycan.* "*I feel as ignored as the fact that giraffe's have green tongues!*"

"Um, they're purple," Serena corrected the angry rock.

"*My point exactly!*"

"Lycan, just stay here," ordered Zade.

"*Yeah, cause I was totally planning to run out on you guys!*"

I reached out and squeezed Serena's hand. "We have no idea what we're about to walk into. You sure you don't want to wait this one out?" I asked her.

"I can do this," she assured me. "I'm here for a reason."

I didn't doubt that. Humans and their gut feelings all the time, am I right?

"All right, then," I nodded. "Let's go do this."

24
ZADE
We all get our butts kicked

If the stories were anything to go off of, Anput's body was buried somewhere here. That, or her stuff was. The stories are different depending on who's telling them, but it's always her in every one.

We quickly made our way to Gallows Hill Park. The closer we got to the park, the more unbearable my headache became. We were in the right place, all right. The source of my nightmare was here.

I looked around at all the people. There were little kids running around playing and adults watching over them, making sure none of them bit another kid. Most of them, children and adults alike, wore cheesy witch costumes complete with pointy hats and broomsticks. There were even black cat costumes. Of course, how original when in Salem. But the rebellious kids wore Transformer or superhero themed costumes. There were few, but they were a mighty few.

You know, the park would be really nice under better circumstances. It had a basketball court, a playground, and at the very end, a baseball field.

I looked up at the sky. The big moon was almost at its peak, and I knew we were running out of nightlight. Man, I loved puns.

Just then, out of the corner of my eye, I spotted a familiar looking couple: Derek and Kyra.

I felt my blood boil inside me. Tunnel vision settled in. "This way," I directed, walking towards the two.

"Ah," smiled Derek. "Glad you're here. Not quite on time, but here nonetheless."

I made a deep throaty growl at him and motioned at my friends. "Get the coin."

Serena unsheathed the knife Juniper had given her earlier today. She gripped it tight in the palm of her right hand.

"No, really," said Derek, "I'm glad you're here. Almost perfect timing, actually. *Almost.*" He pulled a small golden coin from out of his pocket; the same coin I watched Dad give to Kyra when she became alpha.

I sensed something off with Derek. He seemed weirder than usual, almost like he had no conscience. Well... less than before. There was an air about him that radiated unease.

"Speaking of being here," I started, referring to my sister, "When did you... how did you?"

"I killed the old man," was all she said.

I felt all the color drain out of my face. My legs felt wobbly again, and being close to Derek only made my head pound. "You... you killed..."

"A Council member?" Kyra finished. "Yeah."

I, without even a second thought, instinctively felt my hands twitch and morph into long wolf claws. Kyra and Derek did the same.

"Ralph..." uttered Juniper.

Derek flicked me right between my discolored black and blue eyes with his claws.

"What are you *doing*?" I snarled at him.

"Distracting," Derek smiled.

That's when I realized something that was very, very bad, no good whatsoever, terribly horrific and really dreadful:

Kyra was gone.

A muffled scream came from behind me. I turned around and saw Kyra and Serena wrestling for Ralph's knife.

Serena tried with all her might, but the blade was torn from her grasp before anyone could jump in to help her.

I turned to face Derek again. I knew I had to get that coin. I rushed Derek and collided with his body, sending the coin flying up in the air until it landed just inches from my feet. I picked it up and turned to Derek once again, but in his place was a huge, light-brown wolf, and it was gunning right for me.

I did the most reasonable thing I could think of at the moment– I grabbed wolf-Derek by his hind legs, and with all the strength I could muster, threw him to the ground as hard as I could, landing him flat on his back.

The people around him screamed and ran, while a few stopped to take a selfie with us in the background. I hoped that those pictures would be put on the internet so I could see them. Derek probably had the best cheese face a wolf could make.

I would've liked to say that that was the weirdest situation I'd ever been in, but, unfortunately, it wasn't even in the top five. What was, however, was what followed.

Derek flipped himself off the ground, which didn't look easy. That blow to his spine had to hurt.

Derek was a big wolf. Like, huge. But Derek's broken, icy blue stare made him even more frightening.

He barreled towards me, teeth bared. I was paralyzed. I knew I had to do something fast, or I would become Zade-fetti.

When Derek got close enough, I punched him in the snout.

Derek reeled back, howling in pain.

Oh, hell yeah! I punched a wolf in the face, witches! Rock 'n roll!

When Derek recovered, he pounced at me, tearing into my right forearm. I gripped at the tan wolf's neck, trying to pry him off. Jeez, what was this guy— wolf or piranha?

Then, something strange happened. Derek released his death grip on my bloody arm and backed away. I heard my friends' voices in the distance calling for me to watch out, but I wasn't fast enough. I never am, as I've come to find out these past few days.

That's when the most agonizing pain I have ever felt in my life up to this point spread throughout my whole body, starting from between my shoulder blades, reducing me to my hands and knees.

I'd just been stabbed by my own sister, and that made the pain feel even worse.

Maybe I interpreted my nightmare wrong and Kyra kills *me.*

I hung my head and coughed up blood as I lost my grip on the little golden coin that had cost me so much. It looked so unsuspecting, how can it be so important?

At that moment, I felt so betrayed, so deceived, and so, *so* angry.

I felt the heat of my fire leave my tingling fingertips, leaving a trail of blue flames from each clawed hand, climbing, quickly making its way to Derek, enclosing him.

Derek had shifted out of wolf form and made his way towards me, walking at a confident, steady pace down the pathway between my outstretched palms that was untouched by the consuming fire.

I was slipping away from reality. I felt like I was going to die. I looked up at the moon. It was at its peak. It beckoned me; urged me to get up, not to give up, but I didn't even have the strength to stand.

Derek knelt down beside me and lifted my head up with one claw and locked eyes with me. "Time's up," he grinned.

As if I wasn't already in enough pain, he twisted Serena's knife deeper into my back before ripping it out. Derek carefully picked the double-sided coin up from off the blood-stained ground with his long claws and stood up. He stared down at me with a sick, twisted smile on his face.

I wailed in pain and collapsed. I lost all concentration. All around me, I watched as my blue flames died out. Pretty soon, I would too.

Derek studied the fresh blood on the silver blade. He wiped one side of the blade on the palm of his left hand, and did the same with the other. He pocketed the knife and smeared my blood on both sides of the coin.

I felt sick and nauseated at the sight. "You've lost your mind," I growled.

"Oh," smiled Derek. "I've only just found it."

25
SERENA
Never skip leg day

I rushed throughout the park amongst the chaos, trying to direct the swarm of confused and shaken up people to safety when I heard a high-pitched shriek. I immediately knew it was Juniper.

I turned to Oliver who looked even paler than usual, which was a bad sign. "Keep going," I yelled to him over the noisy crowd.

I ran as fast as I could towards the direction of the scream. My muscles ached and I had a gash all the way down my right elbow to my wrist from the tussle with the black-haired, claw-handed girl who I assumed was the sister my friends had talked about previously. But even though my only weapon had been torn from my grasp, I wasn't going to let that stop me from helping innocent people find their lost kids and friends. I pushed past people, occasionally jumping to get a better view and hopefully find Juniper. Then I spotted a glimpse of her blond hair.

When I finally reached Juniper, I found her lying on her side on the ground, struggling to get to her feet.

"Juniper!" I shouted over the commotion.

"I can't get to him!" Juniper screamed, lifting her head to look at me.

"Juniper, get up!" I pulled at her arms, urging her to stand.

"I'm trying!" she yelled. "I physically can't!"

"You can't just give up!" I yelled.

"Serena!"

That's when I noticed huge tears on the side of Juniper's left pant leg and through her leather boots. Her blood almost turned the whole bottom half of her jeans red, and the fabric stuck to the side of her calf.

"Then let me help you," I offered, helping her to her feet. I flung June's left arm over my shoulders, and slowly waded through the people. "What happened?" I asked.

"Kyra. My leg hurts like a *pig*!" growled Juniper. "She somehow managed to grab me by my throbbing calf and ankle, rip into it with her claws and toss me. Pretty sure I rolled my ankle. Or broke it. I don't know, something's just off."

"You'll be fine," I reassured her, "I'm sure of it. We'll all be fine. I have a gut feeling."

26
ZADE
I royally screwed up

I couldn't see my friends through the crowd of people.

I had just been stabbed, and the dominant thought running through my mind was *Oh, no! My shirt! It's ruined!* But then I remembered how short and abrupt William's life as the Zenith was. Could I have the same fate?

Then I just wanted to go back to thinking about how my shirt was going to need a patch.

My stomach churned, my arm hurt, my head throbbed, and my back felt as if it were on fire.

I looked up at Derek and watched as he flipped the coin high up into the air. The little golden coin spun around and around, glowing a brilliant golden color on the front and back, and a deep blue around its curved rim. It lined up with the illuminating blue moon and hung there before falling back down to earth.

Derek caught it. He held the bloody coin tight between his palms. "The blood of Anput!" he chanted. "The blood of Universe! The blood of the omen!"

The blue and golden glow of the coin slowly faded into a gleaming black hue, burning itself into Derek's palms.

Derek screamed and writhed in anguish as a foggy black mist swirled around his body. Just for a split second, his pupil seemed to expand, covering his iris and whites of his eyes in pure black before returning to their normal, light blue color.

It was too late. Whatever that mist was, it wasn't Anput.

Derek dropped the coin, his palms open wide and smoking. The coin's designs had been permanently singed in black into his skin; wolf head on his left, and a hand on his right.

Derek laughed. "I've waited far too long for this moment. You did well, Kyra. I really do love you, please don't forget that." He kissed her.

"Derek," started a nervous Kyra, "What are you talking about?"

Derek grabbed her and held her in a chokehold close to his body. She struggled against him as he pulled the silver knife out of his back pocket and placed the tip of the blade against her chest.

"Derek, you're sick!" Kyra screamed. "You're sick, and I can help you! Let me help you! I'm not ready! I'm not ready to die!"

"I love you and only want to protect you from this cruel and chaotic world. I only want what's best for you," he sympathized. "I'm the Zenith now. I'm the Sky Fire's chosen. It's safe there."

"Derek, please," she pleaded. "Please, please, *please* don't do this to me!" Kyra clawed at Derek, desperately trying to escape his grip.

Derek forced the dagger into her chest, straight through her heart, and then proceeded to shove his hand into her chest cavity, tearing her heart out of her body; the most effective and only way to ensure there would be no chance of survival or coming back for any kind of subspecies.

She fell to the ground, dying, her no longer beating heart beside her on the bloodstained grass.

"KYRA!" I screamed her name. The hair on the back of my neck stood on end, and goosebumps covered every inch of my body as a sound that wasn't entirely my own came out of my scream. It was the Sky Fire, and Kyra was *dying.*

This scream was different than the one I had earlier. That one was a warning– a sign. This time it was the real deal, and I couldn't stop it.

I slowly and painfully crawled towards my big sister. I grabbed her head and wept into her scalp. "Please, no."

"*This*... this is all *your* fault," murmured Kyra with her last dying breath, her eyes fixated on the moon.

"I'm sorry," I apologized. "I'm sorry! I'm sorry!" I whimpered as she went limp in my arms. Tears rolled down my cheeks.

Derek advanced forward, his hands still smoking and a single tear falling down his face. He doesn't have the *right* to cry. HE DOESN'T HAVE THE RIGHT!

He was almost arm's length away from me when my ears started ringing, my headache was cranked up, and my vision blurred. Derek fell to the ground in front of me, hands over his ears and yelling in pain, feeling the same effects as me.

I felt like I was about to pass out. Or die. Whichever came first. Either way, it did not feel good, and my finger tapping was not doing anything to relieve the immense pain.

"Hurts, *doesn't it?*" I snarled at him through gritted teeth.

Derek crawled away from me, still screaming and cursing. The farther away he got, the less my head ached, and it was clear to see that the same went for Derek, too.

"Fine," he surrendered. "I guess I can't kill you without killing myself. He wants you alive, but you will die here anyways. That's fine." Derek stood up, wiping the blood off his upper lip that came from his bleeding nose. "That's fi–"

His sentence was cut short when Oliver the wolf rammed into him, teeth gnashing and claws slashing.

Derek's hands lit up with a pitch-black fire. He grabbed Oliver's neck, catching him on fire, and threw him off, sending him soaring and spiraling through the air.

"Why are you doing this?" I wailed.

"A simple question has stuck with me in my mind for quite a long time now, Zade," said Derek, blood running from the new wound in his neck. "How do you destroy a monster without becoming one? Well, the answer is, quite simply; you don't."

In the background, Oliver had shifted back, and was rolling on the ground, desperately trying to put out the fire stop, drop and roll style.

Next to me, Juniper fell to the ground and wrapped her arms around my neck, just in time to dodge a fireball. The black ball of flames soared over our heads, right into Serena. She fell to the ground, reeling and screaming.

"You've not got long to live, nor much to live for. I'd love to watch the light drain out of your eyes, but I hear sirens. That's my cue to leave. Good luck in the afterlife!"

Derek picked up the bloodstained golden COTA from the ground. He placed it between his palms, the design on each side matching the ingrained designs on his hands, and then melted into the shadows.

That was super odd. Even though it's some kind of black Zenith magic, that's not what the Zenith can do. That's a Shadow thing, and a Shadow thing *only*. He caught the attention of something bad. He wasn't the dark Zenith, he was something else *entirely*.

The fire consuming Oliver and Serena immediately died out, leaving them full of burns.

I clung to my lifeless sister, still sobbing hard and loudly, repeating two worthless words over and over again: *I'm sorry.*

I turned to Juniper and wrapped my arms around her waist, crying into her shirt while she held my head against her body.

I heard police sirens getting louder the closer they got to the park. Great. This was going to be a lot of paperwork.

Then something really bad dawned on me. If the Human police were coming, the Huntsmen had to be nearby, too. After all, a lot of people had seen some pretty shifty things. That's what Derek meant. He knew the police and the Massachusetts Huntsmen would be on their way, so he didn't stick around. This was a huge problem. We had nowhere to go.

A huge, muscular black wolf appeared out of the trees that surrounded the park. His piercing hazel eyes focused on us.

Then the wolf shifted, and in its place now stood an older, muscular African American man, his hazel eyes still fixated on us. He had absolutely no hair on his head.

Not a single strand. He ran towards our group, yelling for us to get up.

After all of my experiences with strangers, I knew better than to up and run off with some random guy, but, once again, I had no choice. I was not going to die today, and neither were my friends. I was still breathing, my heart was still beating, and I had a job to do. I was not going to let my purpose be to die. I was not going to let Derek win. Not as long as I was still alive. Kyra deserved better.

The buff man helped Oliver and Serena to their feet, then picked me and Juniper up, moving us towards the parking lot.

"Oh, buddy," said the man, "You're in tough shape. All of you are. Fortunately, I know just the Shifter to help."

"Any of you know this guy?" asked Serena.

I was in such immense pain that I was unable to speak, but I was able to slightly shake my head.

"I promise I only want to help," reassured the man.

"I'll trust him," said Juniper. "We've got no place else to go."

Serena gasped. "Lycan. We can't forget about him. He's in our car."

"That's perfect. We'll get out of here sooner. Where's your car?" asked muscles.

Serena stumbled into the parking lot, hand in hand with Oliver, burly man in tow dragging Juniper and I with him.

I cried out for my sister, but could do nothing to get to her. I was too badly hurt, and the man's arm was clasped around my lower back and wrapped around my stomach. He had some sort of kung-Fu grip, or something.

"Hurry, they'll be here soon," warned muscles.

"The police?" Oliver coughed.

"Yes, but no. The Huntsmen."

He gently placed Juniper and I in the back seats of the car. Oliver climbed in beside me in the left window seat.

Juniper stroked my cheek and held my hand to calm me down while I rested my head on her shoulder, breathing shakily.

"Zade, listen to me," she demanded. "I need you to listen to me. You're going to be okay. Everything is going to be okay."

"You," said the man, pointing at Serena. "You look to be in the best shape. Get up here."

Serena sat down in the passenger's seat, holding my backpack and the Lycan Stone in her lap.

"Who's this baboon?" demanded Lycan.

"Yeah," said Oliver, "I don't recall you telling us your name."

Muscle man started the engine and pulled out of the parking lot, onto the road. "The name's Reuben Thacher," answered the man, "And I'm going to keep you alive."

Fenrir is here.

About the Author

Hailee Presser lives in a rural community with her mom, dad, and little sister. She was young when her first book was published in 2017, and started writing her books during class when she had had several poems published and decided she wanted to try putting her bigger ideas into the world. She enjoys writing, drawing and designing, and playing music.

www.ingramcontent.com/pod-product-compliance
Lightning Source LLC
LaVergne TN
LVHW091048150826
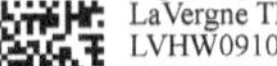
845673LV00002B/496

9798596863574